It felt like heaven to have his arms close around her.

And then, totally unexpectedly, Ran was kissing her, not with the gentle tenderness he had shown her before, but with a fierce sensual passion that took her breath away and with it all her resistance.

He was and always had been a very male man, Sylvie reminded herself. He might not love her, she might not be the woman he wanted, but she was here in his arms, loving him, wanting him, and she could sense how little it would take to overturn his self-control.

Swiftly, dangerously, stabbing right at the heart of her, came the thought that she might not ever have his love, but she could have tonight....

Born in Lancashire, England, PENNY JORDAN now lives with her husband in a beautiful four-teenth-century house in rural Cheshire. Penny has been writing for over fifteen years and now has more than one hundred novels to her name, including the highly successful **To Love, Honor and Betray, Power Games** and **A Perfect Family.** With over sixty million books sold, and transla-tions into seventeen languages, her record is truly phenomenal.

One Night in His Arms develops Ran's and Sylvie's relationship. They first met in an earlier Harlequin Presents® novel, **Fantasy for Two,** when Sylvie developed a teenage crush on her stepbrother's good-looking estate manager.

Books by Penny Jordan

HARLEQUIN PRESENTS®
1941—THE PERFECT SEDUCTION*
1948—PERFECT MARRIAGE MATERIAL*
1954—THE PERFECT MATCH?*
1965—FANTASY FOR TWO
1983—MARRIAGE MAKE UP

and in MIRA® Books
POWER GAMES
A PERFECT FAMILY*
TO LOVE, HONOR AND BETRAY

*Crighton family saga

PENNY JORDAN

One Night in His Arms

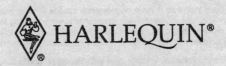

TORONTO • NEW YORK • LONDON
AMSTERDAM • PARIS • SYDNEY • HAMBURG
STOCKHOLM • ATHENS • TOKYO • MILAN • MADRID
PRAGUE • WARSAW • BUDAPEST • AUCKLAND

ISBN 0-373-12002-8

ONE NIGHT IN HIS ARMS

First North American Publication 1999.

PROLOGUE

'WHAT the hell are you doing, Sylvie? Just what kind of game are you playing now?' Ran demanded angrily as he removed her hands, releasing her fingers from his shirt where she had unconsciously curled them in her attempt to get him to listen to what she wanted to say, to understand that she was no longer a child, that she was now completely and totally a woman…a woman who loved and wanted him.

'Ran, this isn't a *game*,' she protested, her eyes starting to fill with anguished tears as he thrust her away. 'I want—'

'Oh, I know exactly what you want, Sylvie,' he interrupted her savagely. 'You want me to take you to bed. But right now what I feel more like doing—' He broke off, said something she couldn't quite catch under his breath and then turned to look at her so that the light fell sharply across his face, outlining the aristocratic arrogance of his profile.

'Your stepbrother is one of my closest friends and my employer and—'

'This doesn't have anything to do with *Alex*,' Sylvie protested frantically. 'This is just between you and me, Ran.'

'You and me? There is no *you and me*,' he told her cruelly. 'You are just a schoolgirl, Sylvie, whilst I am a fully adult man.'

'But Ran, I love you,' Sylvie pleaded desperately,

5

throwing everything she had left into one last attempt to make him see how she felt.

'Really?' Ran drawled mockingly. 'How much? As much as the pop star you were ready to die for six months ago, or the pony you wanted three months before that?'

'That was before I was properly grown up,' Sylvie told him.

So very little space separated them—a few feet…that was all. If she let him walk away from her now without at least trying…

Boldly she closed the distance between them, taking him off guard as she placed her body close to his and wrapped her arms possessively around him, possessively and far too tightly for him to remove them as he had done so easily a few moments ago.

'Ran…' She pleaded with him, lifting her face to him, her mouth trembling. 'Ran, please…'

She felt something that could have been a shudder galvanise his body before clumsily and inexpertly she pressed her mouth against his in a closed-lipped, untutored kiss.

His mouth felt hard and hot, his skin where he had shaved thrillingly rough against her own. Fireworks ignited and exploded deep within her body; her heart was beating so fast she thought she might die of the excitement.

'Ran,' she moaned passionately against his mouth as she twisted with innocent provocation against his body.

Suddenly his own arms were around her, not pushing her away as he had done earlier, but holding onto her, his fingers biting hard into her slender arms as he slid one hand into the back of her hair, holding her head still whilst his mouth started to move on hers.

Sylvie felt her head start to spin and her knees go weak.

If she had thought that her heart was beating fast before, that was nothing to the way it was pounding now. Her whole body ached and pulsed with the intoxication of what was happening.

Ran! Ran! Ran!

She loved him so much, *wanted* him so much. Eagerly she pressed her still coltishly youthful body even closer to his. She could feel every nerve-ending in her skin aching with the intensity of her yearning for him.

The tip of his tongue was caressing the softly swollen outline of her mouth.

She wanted him to make love to her so desperately. These last few weeks, whilst they had been working together clearing the overgrown stagnant lake in the woods on her stepbrother's estate, working on a conservation project which Ran, as her stepbrother's estate manager, had been overseeing, she had come to see him in a new light and in doing so had fallen head over heels in love with him, with all the passion and intensity of her seventeen-year-old nature.

And now, after the corrosive hurt of all his recent rebuffs, all his painful rejections of her attempts to make him realise how she felt, here he was holding her, kissing her…wanting her…

A fiercely sharp thrill of feminine excitement spun through her. Her breasts ached for the touch of his hands, to be held and caressed by him as she had read about, seen in films. The thought of their two naked bodies entwined in the sensual privacy of Ran's bed was almost too much for her. Eagerly she opened her mouth, inviting him to probe deeper with his tongue, but then abruptly, to her shock, Ran was suddenly pushing her away as quickly as he had taken hold of her, his face dark with anger.

'Ran, wh-what is it...what's wrong?' she stammered.

'What's wrong? Oh, for God's sake...' she heard him mutter. 'The fact that you even need to ask that kind of question shows just how... You're a child still, Sylvie... Six months from now...'

She bit down hard on her bottom lip when she saw the irritation in his eyes as he ran his hand through his thick dark copper hair.

'I'm sorry... I should never have done that...' he told her tersely.

Sylvie felt her eyes fill with vulnerable tears.

'You kissed me,' she protested shakily. 'You wanted me...'

'No, Sylvie,' she heard Ran telling her grittily. 'What I wanted,' he told her bluntly, 'was not you, but what you offered. I'm a man, and when a woman comes on to me, offering me sex...' He stopped and shook his head. 'You're a child still, Sylvie.'

'I bet if we were in bed together you wouldn't be saying that,' Sylvie challenged him boldly, adding recklessly, 'I'm not a child at all, Ran, and I could prove it to you...'

She heard the savage hiss as he expelled the air from his lungs.

'Dear God,' she heard him rasp, 'have you the first idea of what you're saying...*suggesting*...?'

'I want you, Ran... I love you...'

'Well, I sure as hell don't want or love you,' he told

her ferociously, his face suddenly shockingly pale underneath its weather-beaten tan. 'And let me give you a small warning, Sylvie: if you continue to go around offering yourself to men, sooner or later one of them's going to take you up on your offer and I promise you that the experience won't be a pleasant one. You're far too young to be experimenting with sex, and when you are old enough it should be with someone of your own age and not... I'm a man, not a boy, Sylvie,' he told her brutally, 'and...well, let's just say that the idea of taking some over-excited and inexperienced little virgin to bed and playing touchy-feely games with her is not my idea of a particularly satisfying relationship—not sexually, not mentally and certainly not emotionally...

'Go and find someone your own age to play with, Sylvie,' he told her grimly.

For a moment Sylvie was tempted to protest, to argue and plead, or even more daringly to throw herself back into his arms and prove to him that she could *make* him want her despite her age and her lack of experience. She was not normally so easily defeated or diminished, but something deep down inside, some very new sense of womanliness, shrank from enduring another rejection from him. And so, instead, swallowing back the tears she was aching to cry, she lifted her head and, tilting her chin to him defiantly, said, 'Yes, I think I will...'

There had been one boy in particular in the party of co-workers involved in the conservation campaign who had shown a very marked interest in her. At the time, newly, wildly in love with Ran, she hadn't paid him very much attention, but now...

A militant sparkle illuminated her eyes. She could see Ran beginning to frown.

'Sylvie,' he warned. Angrily she refused to stop and listen to him, he had no jurisdiction over her.

The bright delicacy of her newly emergent tender love was already tarnishing and fading as resentment, pride and enmity took its place.

Ran!

She loved him but now she felt as though she could very easily come to hate him—she certainly *wanted* to hate him.

CHAPTER ONE

'YOU'RE not serious...'

Sylvie frowned as she studied the synopsis pinned to the front of the file her employer had just handed her.

Lloyd Kelmer the fourth was the kind of eccentric billionaire who, by rights, only ought to have existed in fairy stories—as a particularly genial and indulgent godfather, Sylvie thought. She had been introduced to him at a party to which she had been invited by some acquaintances of her stepbrother's. She had only gone to the party because she had been feeling particularly lost and insignificant, having only recently left her American college and moved to New York. They had got chatting and Lloyd had begun to tell her about the trials and traumas he had experienced in running the huge wealthy Trust set up by his grandfather.

'The old man had this thing about stately homes, I guess I kinda feel the same. He owned a fair handful of the things himself, so he kinda had a taste for them, if you know what I mean. There was the plantation down in Carolina and then a couple of châteaux in France and a *palazzo* in Venice, so it just kinda happened naturally that he should have this idea of using his millions to preserve and protect big houses, and now the Trust has a whole skew of them all over the world, and more wanting to have the Trust bankroll them every day.'

Sylvie, with her own admittedly second-hand experience of her stepbrother's problems in running and financing his own large family estate in England, had quite naturally been very interested in what Lloyd had had to say, but it had still surprised her a few days later to receive not just a telephone call from him but the offer of a job as his personal assistant.

Sylvie wasn't seventeen any longer, nor was she the naive and perhaps over-protected girl she had once been. Lloyd might be in his early sixties and might, so far, not have done or said anything to suggest that he had any ulterior motive whatsoever in making contact with her, but nevertheless, having asked him for time to consider his unexpected offer, the first thing Sylvia had done was telephone her stepbrother in England and ask for his advice.

An unscheduled and unfortunately brief visit from Alex and his wife Mollie to vet Lloyd and talk over the situation with Sylvie had resulted in her deciding to take the job, a decision which, twelve months down the line, she regularly paused to congratulate herself on making, or at least she had done until now.

Her work was varied and fascinating, and barely left her with any time to draw breath, never mind for any personal relationships with members of the opposite sex, but that didn't worry Sylvie. So far, what she had learned from her experiences with men was that she was a particularly poor judge of the breed. First there had been her revoltingly humiliating teenage crush on Ran and his rejection of her, then there had been the appalling danger she had put herself and her family in with her foolish involvement with Wayne.

She and Wayne might never have been lovers but she had known, from the first, of his involvement in the drug scene and, as foolishly as she had tried to convince herself that Ran would fall in love with her, she had also tried to convince herself that Wayne was simply a lost soul in need of protecting and saving.

She had been wrong on both counts. Love was the last emotion Ran had ever felt for her. And as for Wayne… Well, thankfully he was now safely out of her life.

Her new job took every minute of her time and every ounce of her energy. Each new property the Trust decided to 'adopt' had to be inspected, vetted and then painstakingly brought up to the same standard as all the other properties the Trust financed and opened to the general public.

Sylvie knew that her employer's highly individualistic and personalised way of deciding which of the multitude of properties he was offered as potential new additions to the Trust's portfolio were worth acquiring caused other organisations to eye him slightly askance. For Lloyd to accept a house it had to have what he described as the 'right feel', but his eccentricities tended to make Sylvie feel almost maternally protective of him.

Or at least they had until now.

To return from a six-week trip to Prague, where she had been supervising the takeover of a particularly beautiful if horrendously run-down eighteenth-century palace they had recently added to their acquisitions, to discover that in her absence Lloyd had made yet another acquisition in the form of Haverton Hall, a huge neoclassical building set in its own parkland in Derbyshire, had caused her heart to sink into her shoes.

'But Sylvie, this place is a gem, a perfect example of English neoclassicism,' she could hear Lloyd protesting as he studied her stubborn expression. 'I promise you,

you'll love it. I've had Gena book you onto the day after tomorrow's Concorde flight for London. I thought you'd be pleased. You were only complaining way back in the spring how much you wanted to spend more time with your stepbrother and his wife and their son…

'This house… Did I tell you, by the way, that the guy who inherited it just happens to know your stepbrother and that's how he'd got to hear about us? It seems that he was telling your stepbrother about the problems he was experiencing, having unexpectedly inherited this place, and Alex suggested that he should get in touch with me… I wasn't too sure at first. After all, we've already got that pretty little Georgian place down near Brighton, but, well, I kinda felt I owed it to Alex, so I flew over to Britain and went to have a look.'

Sylvie closed her eyes as she listened to Lloyd extolling the virtues of Haverton Hall.

How could she admit to him that it wasn't so much the house itself she objected to as its *owner*?

Its owner…

There it was on the front page of the report… Haverton Hall… Owner… Sir Ranulf Carrington. *Sir* Ranulf now, not just Ran any longer… Not that Sylvie was impressed by a title. How could she be when her own stepbrother was an earl?

She had known all about Ran's unexpected inheritance of course. It had been the subject of a good deal of discussion at Christmas, when she had gone home, not least because Ran, with an estate of his own to run, quite naturally could no longer run her stepbrother's.

No one, least of all Ran himself, had expected that he would inherit. After all, his cousin had only been in his early forties and had seemed perfectly fit. The last thing anyone imagined was that he would suffer a fatal heart attack.

Sylvie had smiled politely, but without interest. The last thing, the last *person* she wanted to waste time talking about was Ran.

Her memories of the way he had rejected her might have been carefully and very deeply buried but...but every time she returned to her brother's home she was painfully reminded of her seventeen-year-old self and her vulnerability.

No question about it, she must have annoyed and aggravated Ran with her unwanted adoration, but surely he could have handled the situation and her a little more gently, let her down a bit more caringly instead of...

Sylvie was aware that Lloyd was watching her expectantly. How could she, as her instincts urged her to do, totally and flatly refuse to have anything to do with Ran? She couldn't. She was a woman now, a woman who prided herself on her professionalism, a woman who along with her outward New York shine and gloss had also developed an inner self-worth and determination. She loved her work and she truly believed that what Lloyd and the Trust were doing was extremely worthwhile.

Secretly, there was nothing she enjoyed more than watching the houses that Lloyd rescued from their often pitiful state of decay being restored to their former glory... Perhaps it was idealistic and, yes, even foolishly romantic of her, but there was something about watching the process, of seeing these once grand homes rising phoenix-like from the ashes of their own neglect, that touched a chord within her. She could well understand what motivated Lloyd, and she suspected that, ironically, it had been that long-ago conservation scheme she had worked on under Ran's supervision which had awakened within her the awareness of how very important it was to preserve and care for—to *protect*—a landscape and its architecture, which had ultimately led to her sharing Lloyd's passion for their task.

However, Sylvie's responsibility as an employee of the Trust included a duty not just to share Lloyd's enthusiasm but to make sure as well that the Trust's acquisitions were funded and run in a businesslike manner, and that the Trust's money was used shrewdly and wisely and not wasted or squandered—a responsibility which Sylvie took very seriously. No project, and certainly no bill, was too small for Sylvie to break down and scrutinise very carefully indeed, a fact which caused the Trust's accountants to comment approvingly on her attention to detail and her excellent bookkeeping.

It had been pointless for Lloyd to protest when they had been renovating the Venetian *palazzo* that he preferred the red silk to the gold which Sylvie had favoured.

'Red is almost twice as expensive,' she had pointed out sternly, adding as a clincher, 'And besides, the records we've managed to trace all indicate that this room was originally decorated in gold and hung with gold drapes...'

'Then gold it is, then.' Lloyd had given in with a sigh, but Sylvie had been the one who had been forced to give in to him a few weeks later when, on their departure from Venice, Lloyd had presented her with a set of the most exquisite and expensive leather luggage crafted as only the Italians could craft leather.

'Lloyd, I can't possibly accept this,' Sylvie had protested with a small gasp.

'Why not? It *is* your birthday, isn't it?' Lloyd had countered, and of course he had been right, and ultimately Sylvie had given in.

Although, as she had told her stepbrother defensively at Christmas when Mollie had marvelled enviously at the luggage, 'I didn't *want* to accept it but Lloyd would have been hurt if I hadn't.' She'd added worriedly, 'Alex, do you think I should have refused…? If you…'

'Sylvie, the luggage is beautiful and you did the right thing to accept it,' Alex had reassured her gently. 'Stop worrying, little one,' he had commanded her.

'Little one'! Only Alex ever called her that, and it made her feel so…so protected and safe.

Protected and safe? She was an adult, a woman, for heaven's sake, and more than capable of protecting herself, of keeping herself safe. Irritably she dragged her attention back to the file she was holding.

'You don't approve, do you?' Lloyd demanded, shaking his head ruefully. 'Just wait until you see it, though, Sylvie. You'll love it. It's a perfect example of…'

'We're already very close to the limit of this year's budget,' Sylvie warned him sternly, 'and—'

'So what? We'll just have to increase this year's funding,' Lloyd told her with typical laid-back geniality.

'Lloyd,' Sylvie protested, 'you're talking about an increase of heaven alone knows how many million dollars… The Trust…'

'I *am* the Trust,' Lloyd reminded her gently, and Sylvie had to acknowledge that he spoke the truth. Even so, she gave him an ironic look to which he responded by informing her loftily, 'I'm just doing what I know the old man would have wanted me to do…'

'By buying a decaying neoclassical pile in the middle of Derbyshire?' Sylvie asked him dryly.

And she was still shaking her head as Lloyd told her winningly, 'You'll love it, Sylvie…I promise you!'

Cravenly Sylvie was tempted to tell him that she was far too busy and that he would have to find someone else to take charge of this particular project, but her pride—the same pride which had kept her going, kept her head held high and her spirit strong through Ran's rejection of her and everything that had followed—refused to allow her to do so.

This time she and Ran would be meeting on equal ground—as adults—and this time…this time…

This time what? This time she wasn't going to let him hurt her. This time her attitude towards him would be cool, distant and totally businesslike.

This time…

Sylvie closed her eyes as she felt the tiny shivers of apprehension icing down her spine. The last time she had seen Ran had been when he had unexpectedly turned up at the airport three years ago when she had been leaving England to finish her degree course in America. She could still remember the shock it had given her to see him there, the shock and the sharply sweet surge of helpless pleasure and longing.

She had still been so vulnerable and naive then, a part of her still hoping that maybe, just maybe, he had changed his mind…his heart… But of course he had not. He had been there simply to assure himself that she was actually leaving the country and his life.

Alex knew, of course, that she had once had a foolish adolescent crush on his friend and employee but, thankfully, that was all he did know; thankfully, he had no knowledge of that shaming and searingly painful, never to be thought about, never mind talked about incident that had taken place when she had still been at university in England.

No one knew about that. Only she and Ran. But that was all in the past now, and she was determined that this time when she and Ran met, as meet they would surely have to, *she* would be the one who would have the upper hand and he would be the one who would be the supplicant; she would have the power to deny and refuse him what he wanted and he would have to beg and plead with her.

Immediately Sylvie opened her eyes. What on earth had got into her? That kind of warped, vengeful thinking was, to her mind, as foolish and adolescent as her youthful infatuation with Ran had been. She was above all that kind of thing. She *had* to be; her job demanded it. No, she would make no distinction between Ran and all the other clients she had had to deal with. The fact that Ran had once cruelly and uncaringly turned down her pleas for his love, for his *lovemaking*, the fact that he had once rejected and demeaned her, would make no difference to the way she treated him. She *was* above all that kind of small-mindedness. Proudly she lifted her head as she continued to listen to Lloyd enthusiastically telling her the virtues of his latest 'find'.

Ran stared grimly around the unfurnished, dusty and cobweb-festooned hallway of Haverton Hall. The smell of neglect and the much more ominous dry rot hung malodorously on the still, late afternoon air. The large room, in common with the rest of the Hall, had a desolate, down-at-heel air of weariness which reminded him uncomfortably of the elderly great-uncle who had owned the property when Ran was growing up. Visits to see him had been something which Ran had always dreaded and, ironically, he could remember how relieved he had been to discover that it was not he but an older cousin who would ultimately inherit the responsibility for the vast, empty, neglected house.

But now that cousin was dead and he, Ran, was Haverton's owner, or at least he had been until a week or so ago, when he had finally and thankfully signed the papers which would convey legal ownership of Haverton and all the problems that went with it into the hands of Lloyd Kelmer.

His initial reaction when he had unexpectedly and unwontedly inherited the place had been to make enquiries to see if any of the British trusts could be persuaded to take it over, but, as their representatives had quickly and wryly explained, the trusts were awash with unwanted properties and deluged with despairing owners wanting them to take on even more.

Faced with the prospect of having to stand aside and watch as the house and its lands fell into an even greater state of decay, Ran hadn't known what on earth he was going to do—his inheritance had been the house and the land; there hadn't been any money to leave for its upkeep—and then Alex had happened to mention the existence of an eccentric American billionaire whose main vocation and purpose in life was the buying up and restoring of old properties which he then opened to the public, and Ran had lost no time in getting in touch with him.

To his relief Lloyd had flown over to England to view the house and promptly declared that he loved it.

That relief had turned to something very different, though, when he had received a fax from Lloyd advising him that his assistant, Ms Sylvie Bennett, would be flying over to Britain to act as his representative over the repair and renovation of the property. He could, of course, have simply chosen to turn his back, walk away, and leave someone else to liaise with Sylvie, but Ran wasn't like that. If he had a job to do he preferred to see it through for himself, no matter how unwanted or potentially problematic that task might be.

Potentially problematic! A bitter half-smile curled his mouth. There was nothing *potential* about the problems that Sylvie was likely to cause him... Nothing potential at all.

He had heard scraps of news about her over the years, of course, mainly from Alex and Mollie. Sylvie had completed her degree course and majored summa cum laude... Sylvie was living in New York and looking for a job... Sylvie had got a job... Sylvie was working in Venice... In Rome... In Prague... Sylvie... Sylvie... Sylvie...

Alex and Mollie weren't his only sources of information, though. Only the previous winter in London, Ran had unexpectedly bumped into Sylvie's mother, Alex's stepmother, predictably just outside Harvey Nichols.

Belinda had gushed enthusiastically over his recent elevation to the peerage. She had always been the most appalling snob and Ran could still remember how bitterly she had opposed Alex's request to her after his father had died that Sylvie be allowed to stay on at Otel Place with him instead of being sent to boarding school.

'Sylvie cannot possibly live with you, Alex,' she had

told him sharply. 'For one thing it simply wouldn't be proper. There is, after all, no blood relationship between you. And for another... Sylvie has been spending far too much time with the wrong sort of people.'

Ran, who had been standing outside Alex's library whilst this conversation had been taking place, had turned round and been about to walk away when, to his disgust, he had suddenly heard his own name mentioned. Alex had demanded of his stepmother, 'What wrong sort of people...?'

'Well, Ran for a start... Oh, I know you count him as one of your friends, but he's still merely an employee and—'

Alex had immediately exploded, informing his step-mother, much to Ran's chagrin, 'Ran *is* a friend and, as for anything else, he happens to be far better born than either you or I.'

'Really?' had come back the acid retort. 'He might be better *born*, Alex, but he still doesn't have any money. Sylvie is very much in danger of developing the sort of crush on him that could totally ruin her reputation if she's to make the right sort of marriage.'

'"The right sort of marriage"?' Alex had retorted an-grily. 'For heaven's sake, what century are you living in...?'

'Sylvie is my daughter and there's no way I want her mixing with the estate workers...and that includes Ran... And whilst we're on the subject, Alex, I really do think that as Sylvie's stepbrother you do have a re-sponsibility to her to protect her from unsuit-able...friendships...'

Ran could still remember how bitterly, *furiously* angry he had been, how humiliated he had felt... He had made sure that he kept his distance from Sylvie after that, even if Sylvie herself had not made that particularly easy. He had been twenty-seven then, ten years older than Sylvie. A man, whilst she was still only a child.

A child... A child who had told him passionately that she loved and wanted him; a child who had demanded even more passionately that he love her back, that he *make* love to her...with her...that he show her...teach her...*take* her...

He could have wrung her pretty little neck for that...wrung it or— He could still remember how she had defied him, flinging herself into his arms, wrapping them round him, pressing her soft lips against him...

Then, he had managed to resist her...*just*...that time...

She had always been so passionately intense. It was perhaps no wonder that the love she had professed to feel for him had ultimately turned to loathing and hatred.

And now she was coming back. Not just to England but here, to Haverton, into his home...his life...

What would she be like? Beautiful, of course; that went without saying... Her mother had told him as much when he had bumped into her—not that he *needed* telling; it had been blindingly obvious even when she was a child that ultimately she would be an extraordinarily beautiful woman.

'You'll know, of course, that Sylvie is working in New York...for a billionaire...' Belinda had cooed happily at him, smiling with satisfaction.

'He's totally besotted with her of course,' she had added, and though it hadn't been put into as many words Ran had gained the distinct impression from Sylvie's mother that the relationship between Sylvie and Lloyd was rather more than that of merely employer and employee...

It had come as something of a shock to him later, when he met Lloyd, to recognise how much older than Sylvie he actually was, but he had told himself that if Sylvie chose to have as her lover a man who was plainly so much older than her then that was *her* business and no one else's.

Sylvie... In another few hours she would be here, their roles in many ways reversed.

'I despise you, Ran, I hate you,' she had hissed at him between gritted teeth when she had first left for New York, averting her face when he had leaned forward to kiss her cheek.

'I hate you...' She had said it with almost as much passion as she had once cried out to him that she loved him. Almost as much...

CHAPTER TWO

FIVE miles or so before her ultimate destination Sylvie pulled the car she had hired at the airport over to the side of the road and switched off the engine—not because she was unsure of where she was going, not even because she wanted to absorb the beauty of the Derbyshire countryside around her, magnificent though it was as it basked warmly in the mid-afternoon sunshine, devoid of any sign of human occupation apart from her own.

No, the reason she had stopped was that she had been tellingly aware for the last few miles not just of the slight dampness of her hands on the steering wheel but, even more betrayingly, of the increasing turmoil of her thoughts and the nervous butterflies churning her stomach.

When she finally met...*confronted*...Ran, she wanted to be calm and in control of both herself and the situation. She was not, she reminded herself sternly, meeting him as an idealistic teenager who had fallen so disastrously and desperately in love with him, but as a woman, a woman who had a job to do. She would not, *must* not allow her own personal feelings to affect her judgement or her professionalism.

In the eyes of other people, her job might appear to be an enviable sinecure, travelling the world, living and breathing the air of some of its most beautiful buildings, able to afford to commission its very best workmen, but there was far more to it than that.

As Lloyd had remarked admiringly to her the previous year, when he had viewed the finished work on the Venetian *palazzo*, Sylvie didn't just possess the most marvellous and accurate eye for correct period detail, for harmony and colour, for the subtlety that meant she could hold in her mind's eye the entire finished concept of how an original period room must have looked, she also had an extremely shrewd and practical side to her nature which ensured that with every project she had worked on so far she had managed to bring the work to completion on time and under budget.

This was something that didn't just 'happen'. It involved hours and hours spent poring over costings and budgets, more hours and hours tramping around warehouses, inspecting fabrics and furniture, and in many cases, because of the age of the houses, it also meant actually finding and commissioning workmen to make new 'aged' copies of the pieces she required. Italy, as she had quickly discovered, was a treasure house for such craftsmen and so, oddly, was London, but always at a price, and Sylvie had surprised herself a little at her ability to haggle and bargain for days if necessary, until she had got what she wanted and at a price she considered to be fair.

This had, of course, led to her often having to take an extremely firm line, not just with the craftspeople she dealt with but very often with the original owners of their properties as well, who very often retained life tenancy in the houses and quite naturally wanted to have their say in how they were restored and furnished.

Oh, yes, Sylvie was used to dealing with sometimes

difficult ex-owners, and situations where she had to use both patience and tact to ensure that no one's pride was hurt.

It was a very definite skill to be able to walk the tightrope between avoiding hurting a prior owner's often sensitive pride and ensuring that the house was restored as she knew Lloyd would want it to be.

But this time it wasn't just the sensitive feelings of a property's ex-owner she was going to need to consider. No, *this* time the person whose feelings, whose emotions were going to need careful handling was herself.

Closing her eyes, she breathed deeply and calmly several times and then opened them again, wiping her hands on a tissue and then re-starting the Discovery's engine.

She had hired a four-wheel drive, not just because she suspected from the plans and other papers Lloyd had given her to study that it would be useful for travelling over the rugged terrain and the no doubt overgrown driveways that surrounded Haverton Hall, but also because, as she had discovered in the past, a large sturdy off-road vehicle often provided a boon for transporting the odd 'find' she came across when scouting around looking for materials for the restoration work to a property.

The statue she had found for the secluded enclosed garden of the Italian *palazzo* had been one such find, bought and paid for on the spot before the vendor could change his mind, and loaded immediately into her car.

Ten minutes later she was driving through the open gates to Haverton Hall. The twin lodges at either side of the gate, joined by a pretty spanning 'archway', had both looked run-down and in need of repair.

Sylvie knew from her homework that they had been constructed at the same time as the main house—and the house, like them, had been designed by one of the country's foremost architects in the Palladian manner favoured by the likes of Inigo Jones.

Theatrically, the drive to the house curved through flanking trees, several of which were missing, spoiling its original symmetry, although those which remained were so heavily in leaf that they still obscured all her attempts to glimpse the house until she had driven past the final curve in the drive.

Sylvie caught her breath. Used as she was to beautiful properties—after all, Alex's ancestral home was renowned for its elegant grace—this one, despite the shabbiness of its fading elegance, was something very special and she could see instantly why Lloyd had fallen so immediately and completely in love with it.

Set on a small incline, so that it could overlook its surrounding gardens and parklands, it was everything that the neoclassicist architects had decreed their houses should be and then some more, Sylvie acknowledged as she drove slowly towards the gravelled parking area in front of the massive columned portico to the house. Stopping the Discovery, she opened the door and started to get out.

Ran had seen her drive up from an upstairs window. She was just a few seconds short of five minutes early. Remembering a younger Sylvie, and her apparent total inability to arrive anywhere on time, he grimaced ruefully to himself before making his way downstairs.

They met on the paved portico. Ran opened the massive front door just as Sylvie mounted the last step. She stopped the minute she saw him, freezing instinctively like a gazelle scenting the presence of a leopard.

He hadn't changed, but then why should he have? He still looked exactly the same. Tall, broad-shouldered, with the smooth warm skin of a countryman, his jeans clinging softly to the taut muscles of his long legs, his forearms bare and bronzed, the soft checked shirt he was wearing exactly the same kind of shirt she could remember seeing him wearing all the years she had been growing up. His hair was still as thick and darkly rich as ever, his jaw just as chiselled—no signs of soft, rich living there, despite the odd snippets of gossip she had picked up from her mother and from Mollie about the discreet parade of elegant, wealthy women who had passed through his life—Ran had always had a penchant for that type, women in the main who were slightly older than himself, *soignée*, knowing…all the things that an adoring, unknowing seventeen-year-old was not.

Only his eyes had changed, Sylvie noticed, with a sudden sharp flicker of sensation which she immediately suppressed. Oh, they were still the same incredible colour, somewhere between onyx and gold, still flecked with those heart-dizzying little specks of lighter colour and still surrounded by those unfairly long, thick dark lashes.

Yes, all that was still familiar to her, but the lazily sensual way they were studying her, the subtle but very male message she could read in them as Ran's gaze flicked over her T-shirt-covered breasts and her slim waist in the plain blue jeans…that was most certainly not familiar to her, at least not from Ran.

And it was only then, when she countered that look with an instinctive and automatically female one of cool

reproval, that Sylvie realised that one of them had closed
the distance between them from its original safe several
metres to a much, much less secure three or four feet.

One of them... To her chagrin Sylvie recognised that
it was not only Ran who had moved so much closer and
that she herself was halfway towards the front door now
instead of on the perimeter of the portico... *When* had
she moved...and how, without knowing what she was
doing...? Ran had always had that kind of effect on
her... *Had* had... All *that* was in the past now, she reminded herself fiercely. And just to ensure that Ran
knew it too she held out her hand to him and, raising
her voice slightly, smiled with cool authority as she
greeted him.

'Ran, good, I'm glad you're here. We can get straight
down to work. I've studied the plans of the house, but I
always find that it makes an enormous difference to actually walk over a property, so...'

God, but she was so incredibly sexy, Ran acknowledged. He could feel the heat, the reaction, the response
surging through his veins. He had been prepared to find
her beautiful. She had always been that. But in the past
it had been almost a sexless, childish kind of beauty...
Now her sensuality, and his own reaction to it, hit him
in the solar plexus like a blow.

As for that cool little voice of authoritative superiority, that distancing little outstretched hand... Later Ran
was to ask himself what on earth he had thought he was
doing and if he had gone completely mad, but at the
time...

Ignoring her outstretched hand, he covered the distance between them and before Sylvie could even begin
to guess what he intended doing his hands were resting

either side of her waist, his scent, his heat filling her
nostrils, his body and his mouth less than inches away
from her own.

'Ran!'

Was that really her own voice, that soft, husky, and,
yes, somehow invitingly sensual little thread of sound,
gasping his name in a slow-drawn-out moan that was
more invitation than protest?

But it was too late to correct the erroneous message
she knew instinctively she had given; Ran was already
acting on what he had obviously interpreted her 'protest'
to mean, his hands lifting from her waist to her arms,
her shoulders, as he drew her closer, his mouth fastening
on hers as he kissed her, not as an old acquaintance or
a friend of her brother's, Sylvie recognised, her senses
reeling, but in all the ways she had dreamed of him
kissing her all those years ago, as a man kissed a woman.

Despairingly she struggled valiantly to resist but it
was useless. Her own foolish senses were doing far more
to aid Ran than to support her, turning traitor and welcoming his sensual assault of her mouth with the eager-
ness of parched land greedily soaking up a heavy rain-
fall.

'Ran…'

She tried weakly to summon her flagging defences,
but the objection she tried to make was lost beneath
Ran's kiss and all the ineffectual parting of her lips did
was to allow Ran's tongue to slip masterfully into the
sweet moistness of her mouth.

Briefly she tried to challenge its entry, but what should
have been the rejecting thrust of her own tongue against
his swiftly became, under Ran's sensually skilful manip-

ulation and expertise, more the intimate sparring of lovers rather than the defensive rejection of adversaries.

'Mmm...' Instinctively Sylvie moved closer, close enough to lean her body fully against Ran's and let his strength support her weakness as delicious tremors of sensation skidded dangerously over her.

'Mmm...'

Beneath her hands Ran's back felt so broad, so firm, so...

Eagerly she tugged his shirt free of his waistband, glorying in the sensation of sliding her hands beneath it and onto the hard heat of his skin.

She felt him shudder responsively as she traced his spine and her own body jolted fiercely in excited reaction.

Beneath her white T-shirt she could feel her suddenly swollen breasts pressing eagerly against her bra. Her nipples ached and even without being able to see them she knew the crests would be hard and erect, the soft flesh around them flooded with aroused dark colour.

Ran could not see what he was doing to her, though...what effect he was having on her as his tongue slid erotically against her own, no longer coaxing but openly, fiercely demanding from her the response his sexuality wanted.

Only one man had seen her body naked and aroused, to only one man had she willingly and, yes, almost wantonly exposed the full femaleness of herself, glorying in her sexuality, in her response to him, her need for him, not fearing...not imagining that he would reject her.

Reject her!

Immediately Sylvie stiffened, her nails momentarily digging into Ran's back as she recognised with shocking abruptness just what she was doing and, even worse, whom she was doing it with.

'Let go of me...' she demanded furiously, fiercely pushing him away, her face bright with mortification and confusion as Ran immediately stepped back from her and then, without taking his eyes off her face, casually unfastened his belt and started to push his shirt back inside his jeans.

If her face had been pink with self-consciousness before, that was nothing to the heat she could feel burning off it now, Sylvie recognised as she refused to give in to the silent visual challenge Ran was giving her and forced herself to keep her gaze locked on his as he slowly and tauntingly completed his task.

Why, oh, why should it be that when a woman disturbed a man's clothing in the heat of passion *he* could make her feel so self-conscious and femininely vulnerable whilst he repaired the dishevelment she had caused, but when it had been a man who had disturbed a woman's clothing *she* was still the one to feel shy and self-conscious when she re-dressed herself?

No wonder the Victorians had considered modesty to be a feminine virtue.

His shirt rearranged to his satisfaction, Ran refastened his belt and then, without taking his eyes off her face, greeted her ironically.

'Welcome to Haverton Hall...'

Sylvie would have given the earth to be able to make a suitably withering response but she could think of none. The shaming fact was that, no matter how she tried to convince herself otherwise, she had done exactly what she had promised herself she would *not* do and allowed him to take the upper hand. And worse than that...far

worse…she had… Quickly she swallowed the frighteningly familiar and painful lump of aching emptiness she
could feel blocking the back of her throat. No way…
She was not going down that road again…not for a
king's ransom. The arrogant, selfish, almost cruel way
Ran had just behaved towards her proved everything she
had ever learned about him. She was under no illusions
about *why* he had kissed her like that… It was his way
of reminding her not just of the past, but also of his
superiority…of telling her that, whilst she might be the
one who was in charge of the project they were going
to be working on together, *he* still had the power to
control her…to control her and to hurt her.

Sylvie turned swiftly on her heel, not waiting for him
to see the emotions she knew were clouding her eyes.

'The lake needs dredging,' she commented crisply as
she shuttered her eyes and stared out towards the large
ornamental lake several hundred yards away from the
house.

It was the wrong thing to say. She could hear the
mocking amusement in Ran's voice as he drawled,
'Well, yes, it does, but let's hope this time you don't
end up head-first in the mud. We'll have to hose you
down out here if you do. There's no way Mrs Elliott is
going to let you into the Rectory smelling of stagnant
lake water and covered in mud and weed…'

Sylvie stiffened, for the moment ignoring his refer-
ence to the ignominious fate which had overtaken her as
an over-eager teenager when she had missed her footing
and fallen head-first into the pond they had been cleaning out on Alex's estate.

'The Rectory?' she questioned him with ominous calm.

She knew from the reports she had read before leaving New York that Ran was presently living in the eighteenth-century Rectory which was part of the estate and which, like the living which had originally gone with it, was in the gift of the owner of the Hall. To judge from the plans and photographs which Sylvie had seen, it was a very, very substantial and handsome property, surrounded by particularly attractive grounds, and she had not been in the least bit surprised to read that it had originally been built for a younger son of the family who had chosen to go into holy orders.

'Mmm...you won't have seen it as you drove in. It's on the other side of the estate. I'm living there at the moment and I've arranged with Mrs Elliott, who used to be my cousin's housekeeper when he lived there, for a room to be prepared for you. Lloyd mentioned that you'd probably be working here for a number of months and he and I agreed that in view of Haverton's distance from the nearest town, and the fact that Lloyd has warned me that you like to keep a very keen eye on the budgets, it makes sense for you to stay at the Rectory rather than waste time and money hunting around for alternative accommodation. Especially since it seems that there could be occasions when you might have to travel abroad to check on work you've set in progress at other Trust properties.'

What he said made sense, but still—she wasn't a child any longer; what she did not need to have was Ran telling her what to do!

'But *you* live at the Rectory,' Sylvie commented quickly.

Immediately Ran's eyebrows rose and he told her laconically, 'It's got ten bedrooms, Sylvie, excluding the upper attics—more than enough space for both of us, I should have thought.'

'Does this Mrs Elliott live in?' Sylvie asked him stiffly.

Ran stared at her for a moment and then burst out laughing.

'No, she doesn't,' he told her coolly, 'although I'm not sure why it should make any difference. You and I have lived under the same roof before, after all, Sylvie, and if it's the thought of any unplanned nocturnal wanderings that's worrying you...' He gave her a wolfish grin and to her fury actually reached out and patted her tauntingly on the arm as he told her, still laughing, 'Don't worry. I'll make sure I get a lock put on my door so that you don't come wandering in...'

Sylvie was too speechless with anger to be able to respond.

'What's wrong now?' Ran challenged her mock-innocently. 'There's no need to be embarrassed at the fact that you occasionally sleepwalk... Of course, it might be an idea to make sure you go to bed wearing something, but I'll warn Mrs Elliott and...'

He stopped as Sylvie made a female growl of frustration deep in her throat.

'That was years ago, when I was a child,' she told him defensively, 'and it only happened once... I don't sleepwalk *now*...'

What was she doing? What was she saying? Why was she letting him do this to her? Sylvie ground her teeth. Yes, once, when she had been initially disoriented and upset at her mother marrying again, she had actually sleepwalked, and might, in fact, have suffered a nasty accident if Ran hadn't happened to see her on his way up to bed. But it had happened *once*, that was all, and, even after she had eventually developed a massive crush on him, surreptitiously creeping into his bedroom had been the last thing on her mind then. She had been far too unworldly, far too naive even to think of such a thing.

'No! Then what are you worrying about?' Ran challenged her, his expression suddenly hardening as he demanded, 'If it's the fact that you'll be living under my roof whilst Lloyd is in New York—'

'*Your* roof?' Sylvie interrupted him quickly, suddenly recognising a way of turning the tables on him and regaining control of the situation, of showing him who was boss. She gave him an acid-sweet smile. 'The Rectory may have *been* yours, Ran, but as part of the estate it is *now* owned by the Trust and—'

'Not so.' Ran stopped her even faster than she had him. 'I have retained ownership of the Rectory and the land. I intend to farm it and to develop the fishing and shooting rights.'

Sylvie was momentarily caught off guard. It was most unusual for Lloyd to allow something like that. He normally insisted on buying whatever land went with a property, if only to ensure that as much of its natural background and surroundings as possible were retained.

'If you'd like to follow me we can drive over to the Rectory now,' Ran offered coolly.

Immediately Sylvie shook her head. 'No... I want to see over the house first,' she told him crisply.

Ran stared at her and then looked at his watch before telling her softly, 'That will take at least two hours, possibly longer; it's now five o'clock in the afternoon.'

Sylvie raised her eyebrows. 'So...?' she challenged.

Ran shrugged.

'I should have thought after a transatlantic flight and the drive here from the airport that you'd have wanted a rest before touring the house, if only so that you can view it with a fresh eye and a clear head.'

'You're out of touch, Ran,' Sylvie told him with a small, superior smile. 'These are the nineties. Crossing the Atlantic for a power breakfast and then re-crossing it for another meeting is nothing,' she boasted.

Ran shrugged again and then waved one hand in the direction of the main doorway as he drawled laconically, 'Very well...after you...'

As he walked towards the door behind her, Ran paused. The sight of her had given him much more of a shock than he liked. He had prepared himself for the fact that he would be meeting her as a woman, and not as the girl he had watched boarding the flight for America, but womanhood came in many different guises and took many different forms. However, none of them could possibly come anywhere near causing the kind of devastating effect on his senses that Sylvie's was creating.

Her hair, long and thick, hung down to her shoulders in an immaculately groomed swathe of molten honey-gold. Just looking at it, at *her*, made him ache to run his fingers through it, to watch its silken weight sliding through his hands...

His stomach muscles tensed. The brilliantly white T-shirt she was wearing hugged the soft shape of her breasts before disappearing into her jeans. The T-shirts he remembered her wearing had been big and baggy and invariably slightly grubby as she happily trotted after him whilst he worked.

Even to his male uneducated eyes, this T-shirt was plainly not the kind one wore to work outdoors in.

And as for her jeans...!

Ran closed his eyes. What was it about the sight of a pair of plain blue jeans lovingly hugging the soft, shapely contours of a woman's behind that had such an evocative, such a provocative effect on a man's male instincts?

Unabashedly he acknowledged that had Sylvie been a complete stranger to him, and had he been walking down the street behind her, he would have instinctively increased his pace to walk past her so that he could see if she looked as good from the front as she did from the rear.

But she wasn't a stranger, she was Sylvie.

'I've told Alex that if you don't keep away from Sylvie he must make you,' Sylvie's mother had once warned him haughtily, shortly after her husband's death.

She had caught Ran at a bad moment and he had reacted instinctively and immediately regretted it as he'd thrown back at her bluntly, 'It's Sylvie you should be warning to keep away from me. She's the one doing the chasing. Teenage girls are like that,' he had added unkindly, watching as Sylvie's mother pursed her lips in shock.

It had been then that he had seen Sylvie slipping past the open doorway of Alex's estate office. Had she overheard them? He'd hoped not. Difficult though her unwanted crush on him sometimes had been, the last thing he'd wanted to do was to hurt her. But now, as he watched her, Ran acknowledged that these days if anyone was going to be hurt it was far more likely to be him! Why had she taken as her lover and her intended partner for life a man more than old enough to be her father? Ran couldn't begin to understand. Unless it was because she had lost her father at such a young and vulnerable age.

Sylvie had pulled open the house's unlocked door and disappeared inside. Sombrely Ran followed her.

CHAPTER THREE

THEY had covered the ground floor of the house, walked
the length of the elegant gallery, with its windows over-
looking the parkland and the distant vista of the
Derbyshire hills, and were just inspecting the enormous
ballroom which opened off it when Sylvie acknowledged
inwardly that Ran might have been right to advise her
to wait until after she had rested to inspect the house.

Haverton Hall's rooms might not possess quite the
vastness of the *palazzo's* marble-floored rooms, nor the
fading grandeur of the Prague palace, but Sylvie had
already lost count of the number of salons and ante-
chambers they had walked through on the lower floor.
The gallery felt as though it stretched for miles, and as
she studied the dusty wooden floor of the ballroom her
heart sank at the thought of inspecting its lofty plasterwork ceiling and its elegantly inlaid panelling. And they
still had the upper floors to go over! But she couldn't
afford to show any weakness in front of Ran and have
him crowing over her. No way. And so, ignoring the
warning beginnings of a throbbing headache, she took a
deep breath and began to inspect the panelling.

'The first thing we're going to need to do is to get a
report on the extent of the dry rot,' she told Ran in a
firmly businesslike voice.

He stopped her. 'That won't be necessary.'

Sylvie paused and turned to look angrily at him.

'Ran, there's something you *have* to understand,' she

told him pointedly. '*I* am in charge here now. I wasn't asking for your approval,' she told him gently. 'The house has dry rot. We need a specialist's report on the extent of the damage.'

'I already have one.'

Sylvie started to frown.

'When...?' she began.

But before she could continue Ran told her coolly, 'It was obvious that the Trust would need to commission a full structural survey of the place to assess it, so in order to save time I commissioned one. You should have had a copy. I had one faxed to the Trust's New York office last week when I received it.'

Sylvie could feel her heart starting to beat just a little bit too fast as the angry colour burned her face.

'You commissioned a survey?' she questioned with dangerous calmness. 'May I ask who gave you that authority?'

'Lloyd,' came back the prompt and stingingly dismissive reply.

Sylvie opened her mouth and then closed it again. It was quite typical of Lloyd that he should have done such a thing and she knew it. He would only have been thinking of saving time in getting his latest pet project under way; he would not have seen, as she so clearly did, that what Ran was actually doing was not trying to be helpful but deliberately trying to upstage her and challenge her authority.

'I take it you haven't read the report,' Ran was continuing, talking to her as though she were some kind of errant pupil who had failed to turn in a piece of homework, Sylvie decided as she silently ground her firm white teeth.

'I haven't received any report to read,' she corrected him acidly.

Ran shrugged.

'Well, I've got a copy here. Do you want to continue with your inspection or would you prefer to wait until you've had a chance to read through it?'

Had the question been put by anyone else, Sylvie knew that she would have gratefully seized on the excuse to defer her self-imposed task until after she had had a rest and the opportunity to do something about the increasingly painful pressure of her headache, but because it was *Ran* who asked her, *Ran* whom she was fiercely determined not to allow to have any advantage over her, she shook her head and told him aggressively, 'When I want to change any of my plans, Ran, I'll let you know. But until I do I think you can safely take it that I don't…'

She saw his eyebrows lift a little but he made no comment.

It had been a hot week and the air in the ballroom was stifling, the dust thick and choking as it lay heavily all around them.

Sylvie sneezed and winced as the pounding in her head increased. The bright early evening sunlight streaming in through the windows was making her feel oddly dizzy and faintly nauseous… She tried to look away from it and gave a small gasp of pain as the act of moving her head made the blood pound agonisingly against her temples.

Only rarely did she suffer these enervating headaches. They were brought on by stress and tension. Turning away so that Ran wouldn't see her, she tried to massage the pain away discreetly.

'Careful…' Ran warned her tersely.

'What?' Sylvie spun round, colour flaring up under her skin as Ran motioned towards a piece of fallen plasterwork she had almost walked over.

She was feeling increasingly sick and dizzy in the sharp bright light. Despairingly she closed her eyes and then wished she hadn't as the room started to spin dangerously around her.

'Sylvie…'

Quickly she opened her eyes.

'You're not well; what is it?' she heard Ran demanding tersely.

'Nothing,' she denied angrily. 'A headache, that's all.'

'A *headache*…?' His eyebrows shot up as Ran studied her now far too pale face and saw the tell-tale beading of sweat on her forehead.

'That's it,' he told her forcefully. 'We can finish this tomorrow. You need to rest.'

'I need to do my job,' Sylvie protested shakily, but Ran quite obviously wasn't going to listen to her.

'Can you make it back to the car?' he was asking her. 'Or shall I carry you?'

Carry her… Sylvie gave him a furiously outraged look.

'Ran, there's nothing wrong with me,' she lied, and then gave a small gasp as the quick movement of her head as she shook it in denial of his suggestion caused nauseating arrows of pain to savage her aching head.

The next thing she knew, Ran was taking her very firmly by the arm and propelling her towards the door, ignoring her protests to leave her alone.

At the top of the stairs, to her infuriated chagrin, he turned round and swung her up into his arms, telling her through gritted teeth, 'If you're going to faint on me, Sylvie, then here's the best place to do it.'

She wanted to tell him that fainting was the last thing she intended to do, but her face was pressed against the warm flesh of his throat and if she tried to speak her lips would be touching his skin and then...

Swallowing hard, Sylvie tried to concentrate on banishing the agonising pain in her head but it was something that she couldn't just will away. As she knew from past experience, the only way of getting rid of it was for her to go to bed and sleep it off.

They were downstairs now and Ran was crossing the hallway, thrusting open the door and carrying her out into the fresh air.

'What are you doing?' she demanded as he walked past her Discovery towards his own car.

'I'm taking you home...to the Rectory,' he told her promptly.

'I can drive,' Sylvie protested, but to her annoyance Ran simply gave a brief derogatory laugh.

He told her dismissively, 'No way...' And then she was being bundled into the passenger seat of a Land Rover nearly as ancient as the one she remembered him driving around her stepbrother's estate, and as she struggled to sit up Ran was jumping into the driver's seat next to her and turning the key in the ignition.

'Ran...my luggage...' She was protesting, but he obviously had no intention of listening to her. With the Land Rover's engine noise making it virtually impossible for her to speak over it, Sylvie gave up her attempt to stop him and subsided weakly into her seat, hunching her shoulders as she deliberately turned her head away and refused to look at him.

As he glanced at her hunched shoulders and averted profile, Ran's frown deepened. In that pose she looked so defenceless and vulnerable, so different from the professional, high-powered businesswoman she had just shown herself to be and much more like the girl he remembered.

The Land Rover kicked up a trail of dust as he turned off the drive and onto the track that led to the Rectory.

Girl or woman, what did it matter so far as *he* was concerned? He cursed under his breath, his attention suddenly caught by the sight of several deer grazing placidly beside the track. They were supposed to be confined to the park area surrounding the house and not cropping the grazing he needed for his sheep. There must be a break in the fence somewhere—the new fence which he had just severely depleted his carefully hoarded bank balance to buy—which meant... There had been rumours about rustlers being in the area; other farmers had reported break-ins and losses.

Once he had seen Sylvie settled at the house he would have to come back out and check the fencing.

Sylvie winced as the Land Rover hit a rut in the road, sitting up and just about managing to suppress a sharp cry of pain—or at least she thought she had suppressed it until she heard Ran asking her curtly, 'What is it? What's wrong?'

'Nothing... I've got a headache, that's all,' she stressed offhandedly, but her face flushed as she saw the look he was giving her and she realised that he wasn't deceived.

'A headache?' he queried dryly. 'It looks more like a migraine to me. Have you got some medication for it or...?'

'It isn't a migraine,' Sylvie denied, adding reluctantly, 'It's… I… It's a stress headache,' she admitted in an angry rush of words. 'I…I get them occasionally. The travel…flying…'

Ran's mouth hardened as he listened to her.

'What's happened to you, Sylvie?' he asked her quietly. 'Why should it be so difficult for you to admit to being vulnerable…human…? What *is* it that pushes you, drives you, forces you to make such almost superhuman demands on yourself? Anyone else, having flown across the Atlantic and driven close on fifty miles without a break, would have chosen to rest and relax a little bit before starting to work, but not you…'

'That may be the British way, but it's different in America,' Sylvie told him sharply. 'There, people are rewarded, praised, for fulfilling their potential and for—'

'Driving themselves into such a state of exhaustion that they make themselves ill?' Ran challenged her. 'I thought that Lloyd was supposed to…' He stopped, not wanting to put into words, to make a reality, the true relationship he knew existed between Sylvie and her boss. 'I thought he cared about you…valued you…' he finished carefully instead.

Sylvie was sitting upright now, ignoring the pounding pain in her head as she glared belligerently at Ran.

'Lloyd doesn't…he isn't…'

She stopped, shaking her head. How could she explain to Ran of all people about the thing that drove her, the memories and the fears? As a teenager she had done so many foolish things, and even let down the people who had loved and supported her; her involvement with Wayne was something she knew she would always regret.

She hadn't known at the time, of course, just what he was. In her innocent naiveté she had never guessed that he was anything other than someone who had bought a handful of recreational drugs to pass on to people at rave parties.

When she had run away from university, though, to join Wayne and the band of New Age travellers who had invaded her stepbrother's lands, she had quickly learned just what a mistake she had made, and she knew that she would always be grateful to Alex and his wife Mollie, not just for the fact that they had helped her to extricate herself from a situation she had very quickly grown to fear, but also for the fact that they had supported her, believed in her, *accepted* her acknowledgement that she had made a mistake and given her the opportunity to get her life back on track.

She and Wayne had never actually been lovers, although she knew that very few people would believe that, nor had she ever used drugs; but she *had* been tainted by his lifestyle, *had* had her eyes opened painfully to certain harsh realities of life, and after Alex had interceded for her with her mother and with the university authorities, getting her a place at Vassar where she had been able to complete her education, she had promised herself that she would pay him and Mollie back for their kindness and their love and support by showing the world and her detractors just how worthy of that support she was.

At Vassar she had gained a reputation as something of a recluse and a swot; dates and parties had been strictly out of bounds so far as she was concerned and her dedication had paid off with excellent exam results.

And now, just as she had once felt the need to prove

herself to Alex and Mollie, she felt a corresponding need to prove herself worthy of Lloyd's trust in her professional abilities. It was true that sometimes she did drive herself too hard...but the scornful verbal sketch of herself that Ran had just drawn for her quite illogically hurt.

Given that she had striven so hard to be considered wholly professional, to be capable and strong, it was quite definitely illogical, she knew, to wish forlornly that Ran might have adopted a more protective and less critical attitude towards her, that he might have shown more concern, some tenderness, some...

'Why the hell didn't you *say* you weren't feeling well?'

Ran's curt demand broke into her thoughts, underlining their implausibility, their stupidity, their dangerous vulnerability.

'Why should I have done?' Sylvie countered defensively, adding tersely, 'I hardly think that either the Trust or the owners of the properties it acquires would thank me for wasting both time and consequently money by bringing up the subject of my own health during business discussions. You and I may know one another from the past, Ran, but so far as I am concerned the fact that we have dealings with one another in the present is entirely down to the business and professional relationship between us.'

It was several seconds before Ran bothered to respond to her unrehearsed but determinedly distancing little speech, and for a moment Sylvie thought that he was actually going to ignore what she had said, but then he turned towards her and said, 'So what you're saying is that it's to be purely business between us, is that it?'

It took every ounce of courage that Sylvie possessed,

and then some, for her to be able to meet the look he was giving her full-on, but somehow or other she managed to do so, even if the effort left her perilously short of breath and with her heart pounding almost as painfully as her head, She agreed coolly, 'Yes.'

Ran was the one to look away first, his face hardening as he glanced briefly at her mouth before doing so.

'Well, if that's what you want, so be it,' he told her crisply, returning his attention to his driving.

His response, instead of making her feel relieved, left her feeling... What? Disappointed that he hadn't challenged her, hadn't given her the opportunity to...to what? Argue with him? Why should she *want* to? What was it she felt she had to prove? What was it she wanted to be given the opportunity to prove?

Angry with herself, Sylvie shook her head. There was nothing, of course. She had made her point, said what she wanted to say and now Ran knew exactly how she viewed their working relationship and exactly how she viewed him. He could be in no doubt that, were it not for the fact that he was the owner of a property the Trust had decided to acquire, she would have no cause, nor any wish, to be involved with him.

Up ahead of her she could see a grove, a small wooded area; Ran drove into it and through it towards the mellow high red-brick wall and through its open gates.

The house which lay beyond them took Sylvie's breath away.

She was used to grand and beautiful properties, to elegance of design, to scenery and settings so spectacular that one had to blink and look again, but this was something else.

This was a house as familiar to her as though she had already walked every one of its floors, as though she knew each and every single one of its rooms, its corners. This was a house, *the* house she had created for herself as a girlhood fantasy. A house, *the* house, the *home* which would house and protect the family she so much longed to be a part of.

Totally bemused, she couldn't drag her gaze away from its red-brick walls, her professional eye automatically noting the symmetrical perfection of its Georgian windows and the delicacy of the pretty fanlight above the doorway. An ancient wisteria clothed the facing wall, its trunk and branches silvery grey against the rich warmth of the brick; its flowering season was now over but its soft green tendrils of leaves were coolly restful to her aching eyes.

Prior to her mother's second marriage to Alex's father, they had lived in a smart apartment in Belgravia—her mother had been a very social person, involved, as she still was, in a good many charities and a keen bridge player, but Sylvie had never really felt comfortable or at home in the elegant London flat. Before his death her father had owned a large house in one of London's squares and Sylvie still missed the freedom that living there had given her.

To comfort herself she had created her perfect house and the perfect family to go with it, mother, father, daughter—herself, plus a sister for her to play with and a brother too, along with grandparents and aunts and uncles and cousins. It had been the house that she had given most of her mental energy and imagination to lovingly creating, though. A house for a family, a house that wrapped itself lovingly and protectively around you…a house with enough land for her to have a pony. A house… The house… *This* house..!

Ran had stopped the Land Rover. Shakily she got out, unable to take her eyes off the house, barely aware of Ran's expression as he watched her.

Just for a second, seeing that luminous bemused expression on her face, he had been transported back in time…to a time when she had looked at *him* like that, a time when…

Grimly he reminded himself of what Sylvie had just said, of the terms she had just set between them. She had made it more than plain, if he had needed it underlining, which he had not, that the only reason she was here in his life was because of her job and that, given the choice, she would far rather be working alongside someone else…*anyone* else.

The gravel crunched beneath Sylvie's feet as she walked slowly, as if in a dream, towards the Rectory's front door.

Already she knew what would lie beyond it—the soft-toned walls of the hallway with its highly polished antique furniture, its glowing wooden floors, its rugs and bowls of country-garden flowers. In her mind's eye she could see it all as she herself had created it, smell the scent of the flowers…see the contented look in the eyes of the cat who basked illegally on the rug, lying there sunning himself in a warm beam of sunshine, ignoring the fact that his place and his basket were not here but in the kitchen.

Automatically her hand reached out for the door handle and then she realised what she was doing. Self-consciously she stepped back, turning her head away so that she didn't have to look at Ran as he stepped past her to unlock the door.

It was cruelly ironic that Ran, of all people, should own this house that so closely epitomised all that she herself had longed for in a home as a young girl.

The front door was open. Ran paused to allow her to precede him inside but, as she did so, Sylvie came to an abrupt halt. Faded, unattractive wallpaper and chipped dark brown paint assaulted her disbelieving gaze. In place of the polished mellow wooden floor she had expected was a carpet, so old and faded that it was no longer possible to even guess at its original colour, but Sylvie suspected with disgust that it must have been the same horrendous brown as the paintwork.

True, there was some furniture, old rather than antique, dusted rather than polished, but there were certainly no flowers, no perfumed scent, nor, not surprisingly, was there any cat.

'What is it?' Ran asked her.

Hard on the heels of the acute envy she had felt when she had first seen the exterior of the house came a pang of sadness for its inner neglect. Oh, it was clean enough, if you discounted the air possessing a sharp, almost chemical smell that made her wrinkle her nose a little, but it was a long, long way from the home she had so lovingly mentally created.

She heard Ran moving around in the hall behind her.

'I'll take you up to your room,' he told her. 'Have you got something for your headache?'

'Yes, but they're in my luggage which is in my hire car,' Sylvie told him grimly.

In the excitement of seeing the house her headache

had abated slightly, but now the strong smell in the hallway had made it return and with interest. She could no
longer deny that lying down somewhere dark and quiet
had become a necessity.

'It's this way,' Ran told her unnecessarily as he
headed towards the stairs.

Once they might have been elegant, although now it
was hard to know; the original staircase no longer existed and the monstrosity which had replaced it made
Sylvie shudder in distaste.

The house had a sad, forlorn air about it, she recognised as she reached the large rectangular landing, car-
peted again in the same revolting dun-brown as the hallway below.

'Did your great-uncle live here?' Sylvie asked him
curiously.

'No. It was let out to tenants. When my cousin inherited he moved in here, and after his death... I thought
about selling it, but it's too far off the beaten track to
attract the interest of a buyer, and then once I'd made
the decision to hang onto the land and farm it seemed
to make sense to move into the house myself. It needs
some work doing on it, of course...'

Sylvie said nothing but her expressive eyes gave her
away and Ran continued coldly, 'Well, yes, I can see
that to someone such as yourself, used to only the very
best that money can provide, it must be rather a come-
down. I'm sorry if the only accommodation I can offer
you isn't up to your usual standards...' Ran's eyes darkened as he reflected on the elegance of Alex's home and
the luxury she must have enjoyed with Lloyd, but to
Sylvie, who was remembering how Ran had once seen
her living in the most basic and primitive conditions,

when she had been part of the group of New Age travellers who had set up camp on Alex's estate, the look he was giving her seemed to be one of taunting mockery.

'You're down here,' Ran was saying as he led the way down a corridor with doors off either side of it, pushing one of them open and then standing to one side as he waited for her to enter.

The bedroom was large, with two long windows that let in the glowing evening sunlight. The old-fashioned wooden furniture, like the tables in the hallway, was spotlessly clean but lacked the warm lustre that it would once have had from being lovingly polished by several generations of female hands. The empty grate in the pretty fireplace, which she would have filled with a collection of dried flowers or covered with an embroidered firescreen, was simply that—an empty grate. The curtains and the bedding were modern and, she suspected, newly purchased for her visit. The same depressing brown carpet as downstairs covered the floor.

'You've got your own bathroom,' Ran told her as he crossed the floor to push open another door. 'It's old-fashioned but it works.'

As she looked into the bathroom past him, Sylvie said wryly, 'It may be old-fashioned to you, Ran, but this type of plain white Edwardian sanitaryware is very much in vogue right now.'

'There are wardrobes and cupboards on that wall,' he told her unnecessarily, indicating the bank of built-in furniture. 'I haven't had the chance yet, but tomorrow I'll bring up a desk from downstairs.'

'I'll certainly need somewhere to put my laptop,' Sylvie agreed. 'But I will also need to have a room somewhere, I think preferably up at the Hall itself, to work officially from. But that's something we can discuss later.

'Where's your housekeeper?' she asked him. 'I'd like to meet her…'

'Mrs Elliott… She'll be here in the morning. I can introduce you then.

'Look.' He glanced at his watch and then told her, 'I'm afraid I'm going to have to leave you. I have to go out, but if you'd like something for that headache…'

'What I'd like is my own medication,' Sylvie told him acidly, 'but, since that's not available, thanks but no, thanks. I need my luggage,' she added pointedly.

'If you give me the keys to your Discovery, I'll go and get it for you,' Ran told her promptly. 'Just give me ten minutes to make a couple of phone calls.'

As she handed over the keys to her car Sylvie wondered where it was he was going to be spending the evening and with whom.

Ran was a very masculinely attractive man; even she had to admit that.

'I doubt that Ran will ever marry,' Alex had once commented.

'Why not?' Sylvie had questioned curiously, her adoring teenage heart thumping frantically at the thought of being married to Ran, of being his wife, of sharing his life, his *bed*… A delicious shiver of anticipatory pleasure had run through her as she'd willed her stepbrother to say that there was a mysterious someone in Ran's life, far too young for him as yet, a special someone… herself…

But instead, disappointingly, prosaically, Alex had told her, 'An estate manager's salary and tied accommodation in a small cottage are hardly up to the standard or style of living that the women Ran dates are used to, and he's far too proud to want to live off his wife…'

'The women…?' Sylvie had flared unhappily, whilst her mother, who had been listening to their conversation, had chipped in disparagingly.

'Ran would be far better off marrying some farmer's daughter, a girl who's been brought up for that kind of lifestyle…'

Sylvie remembered how Alex's eyebrows had risen at this display of snobbery from her mother. But now, of course, Ran's prospects had changed. She knew how much Lloyd had paid him for the house and the estate. There had been death duties and other commitments to meet, of course, but even so he would have been left with a sizeable sum, much larger than the inheritance she had received from her father, which her over-anxious mother had been convinced would make her a target for potential fortune-hunters.

Yes, with the money he had at his disposal, and the living he would no doubt make out of the land, Ran would financially have a great deal to offer a woman.

Not that a man's financial status had ever counted for anything with her. Love in a cottage might be an ideal, a daydream, a fantasy now relegated to her childhood, but secretly Sylvie still adhered to the belief 'Better a humble home where love is than a mansion without it'— and, of course, there had never been any doubt in her mind whatsoever that when it came to the material things in life what Ran had to offer the woman he loved…

The woman he loved.

She bit her lip as Ran started to walk away from her. Once he had gone she stared out of the bedroom window. It overlooked the formal gardens to one side of the house. Like the house, they had an air of neglect; of being unloved. Sylvie's vivid imagination soon filled the neglected borders with lush herbaceous plants and restored the overgrown rose garden to what must have been a haven of peace and perfume.

The air in the bedroom felt stale, but when she tried to open one of the sash windows all she managed to do was to break one of her nails. Cursing herself under her breath, she winced as the pain inside her head increased. Perhaps she had been rash in refusing Ran's offer of some headache tablets.

Quickly she opened the bedroom door and hurried back down the stairs.

She found Ran in a huge ill equipped kitchen at the back of the house. As she pushed open the door he was heading towards it carrying a tray of tea.

'Who's that for?' Sylvie demanded suspiciously.

'You,' Ran told her promptly. On the tray Sylvie could see a small packet of a familiar brand of headache tablets. The temptation to tell him that she didn't want either his tea or his tablets was so strong that she had to fight hard to ignore it. Where on earth had such perversity come from—and when she had come downstairs especially to ask him for them?

'I can manage it for myself,' she told him ungraciously, and she held out her hands for the tray. The look he gave her made her flush but doggedly she stood her ground. Even so, she doubted that he would have handed the tray over to her if the telephone in the hallway had not rung.

As he went to answer it Sylvie headed for the stairs.

'Vicky...' she heard him saying warmly, and then, 'Yes...it's still on... I'm looking forward to it too,' he confirmed, his voice dropping and deepening. 'Look, I have to go...'

Sylvie was halfway up the stairs when she heard him replacing the telephone receiver.

'Sylvie—' he began.

But she cut him short, turning round and telling him crisply, 'Don't let me delay you if you've got a date, Ran. I've got plenty of work to read up on.'

'You need to sleep off your headache,' Ran told her curtly.

'On the contrary. I need to work,' Sylvie corrected him sharply as she continued on her way upstairs.

Ran stood and watched her. God, but she got under his skin. Why did he let her? Why hadn't he simply told her that the only date he had this evening was with a damaged fence?

Angrily he turned on his heel and strode towards the front door.

As he closed it behind him Sylvie's body slumped slightly; tension had invaded each and every one of her muscles and it wasn't just her head that pounded with stress now, it was her whole body. Wearily she made her way to her bedroom, took two of the tablets, drank her tea and then, having removed her outer clothes, crawled into bed in her underwear. It was only when she was on the verge of sleep that she remembered that she had neglected to ask Ran to do something about the window she had been unable to open.

CHAPTER FOUR

RAN grimaced as he studied the very obviously cut-through pieces of fencing wire. No accident, that. Someone had quite definitely used wire cutters on them, which meant...

The lambs which had been born early in the spring had all gone now, his breeding stock the only flock that remained. It was an unpalatable thought though, that the deer roaming the home park made a tempting target for rustlers, all the more so because those animals were tame and not used to being hunted.

The last time he had seen Alex, the two of them had discussed the pros and cons of tagging their deer. Like him, Alex had a small herd on his estate, but since their marriage Mollie, his wife, had added a new strain to them in the shape of the same miniature deer that the Duchess of Devonshire had bred so successfully.

As Ran glanced towards the ha-ha which separated the parkland from the main gardens to the Hall he could hear the peacocks screeching their warning that someone was approaching the house.

Frowning, he got up, dusting the twigs and grass from his jeans as he headed back to the Land Rover.

It was almost ten o'clock, hardly the time for anyone to be visiting the Hall for any legitimate reason. Still frowning, he started the Land Rover's engine.

Sylvie had woken up abruptly, wondering where on earth she was and why she couldn't breathe properly.

The dying sun had heated the already stuffy air in her bedroom to the point where she could actually taste its staleness in her mouth. The sharp intensity of her earlier headache had, thankfully, eased, but she knew there was no guarantee of its not returning if she continued to breathe such unhealthy air.

What she needed was some fresh air. After sluicing her face with cold water she pulled on her jeans and T-shirt, grimacing slightly as she did so. New York had effected some changes in her, she reflected wryly. Once she would have been quite happy in grubby clothes, but now...

Lloyd often teased her for the preppy look of loafers, jeans and white T-shirts which had become her trademark, but, as she had loftily told him, they made good sense for her job in that they always looked workmanlike and enabled her to climb scaffolding and straddle platforms whilst at the same time looking smart and businesslike enough to command the respect of the sometimes very chauvinistic men she had to deal with. Women too, especially in Italy, the home of style with a capital S, had been discreetly impressed with her working 'uniform', she had noticed. Now it was second nature to her always to wear immaculate white T-shirts and equally immaculate jeans, and the act of putting on clothes she had already been wearing all day was not one she enjoyed.

She had a spare set of car keys in her purse—another trick she had learned from her work. Spare keys to anything and everything were a necessity, as she had quickly discovered the first time she had allowed one of the workmen to accidentally lock her out of a building

and then go home with the keys—it would be a simple
enough matter for her to walk back to Haverton Hall and
pick up her Discovery. The last thing she wanted was to
be dependent on Ran for a lift to the place in the morning, and besides—a small triumphant smile curved her
full mouth—it would be good to be able to point out
haughtily to him that whilst he had been out enjoying
himself with his girlfriend *she* had been working.

She had a well-developed sense of direction and the
walk to the Hall, which someone else might have found
a daunting prospect, was nothing to her.

Humming happily to herself, Sylvie set out.

It was a warm summer's evening, with just enough
remaining light for her to avoid the occasional cloud of
midges hovering on the still air.

Being on foot gave her the opportunity to assess the
land far better than she had been able to do from inside
Ran's Land Rover. She had spent enough time on Alex's
estate to appreciate that it was going to take a consid-
erable amount of good husbandry on Ran's part to bring
this land into the same productive state as her stepbrother's. Oddly, she envied him the challenge, but not
so much as she envied his wife the pleasure she would
have in lovingly restoring the Rectory; in making it the
home that Sylvie knew it could be. Oh, yes, she envied
her that.

Only that? Sylvie paused, shaking her thick hair back
from her head. Of course only that. She couldn't possibly envy her Ran, could she—Ran and the children he
would give her? No, of course she couldn't.

It was almost dark when Sylvie eventually reached the
Hall, its bulk throwing long shadows across the gravel,

cloaking both her and the Discovery as she walked towards it.

The sound of other feet on the gravel momentarily
made her freeze until she recognised the familiar shapes
of half a dozen inquisitive peacocks and peahens. The
cocks were sending their shrill cries of warning up into
the still night air.

Sylvie laughed as she heard them, relieved, and shook
her head at them as she told them cheerfully, 'Yes, I
may be an intruder now, but you're going to have to get
used to me. You and I shall be seeing an awful lot of
one another, you know.'

She stayed with them for several minutes, watching
them and talking to them. Soon, no doubt, when it became fully dark, they would be roosting somewhere out
of the way of any predatory hunting foxes.

Turning her back on them, Sylvie stared thoughtfully
at the house, trying to visualise how it would look once
the stone had been cleaned. That alone would cost a
small fortune and would, no doubt, take almost as long
as it would take for the interior to be renovated. She
must ask Ran to give her any formal records from when
the hall had originally been built and the work done on
it since then. She wasn't sure, but she suspected that the
stairway she had seen had been, if not the work of
Grinling Gibbons, then certainly the work of one of his
more innovative apprentices.

The tiny sprays of coral, the seashells and unbelievably realistic fish carved into the wood related, no doubt,
to the fact that the money for the original house had
come from the very profitable overseas trading its owner
had been involved in. As a prominent member of King

Charles II's court, and one of his favourites, he undoubt-
edly had had access to many money-making activities.

Idly Sylvie wondered what it would have been like to
live in such a time and in such a house. It was one of
her indulgences that whenever she became involved with
a new property she couldn't help daydreaming about its
past, its history, picturing herself as part of it...
imagining how and what she would have chosen had she
been its chatelaine and then translating that into...

Ran parked his Land Rover out of sight and sound of
the house. The peafowl, on their way to their roosting
place, saw him and started to flap their wings until he
threw down the grain he had brought with him to silence
them. No point in giving the intruders the same warning
he himself had so helpfully received.

Abandoning her study of the Hall, Sylvie stepped back
into the shadows and made her way back towards her
parked car. As he rounded the corner of the building, for
a moment Ran thought that its frontage was deserted,
and then he saw someone moving in the semi-darkness.

Immediately he acted, crouching down low and using
the shadows to conceal his presence as he ran light-
footed and quietly towards Sylvie's car and whoever it
was who was trying to break into it. There wasn't any
time to waste—the Discovery's driver's door was already open. Launching himself towards the figure about
to climb into it, Ran brought the thief down in a rugby
tackle, pinning him down on the ground beneath him as
he grunted, 'Got you.'

Sylvie didn't see her assailant spring out at her but
she certainly felt him as the speed of his attack carried
her to the ground, his weight keeping her there as his
hands moved quickly and lightly over her body.

Frantically she tried to struggle, kicking out at him, clawing his back as he pinned her legs, imprisoning her beneath his own, and then reached out to imprison her hands. As she twisted and turned beneath him, trying to throw off his weight, Sylvie felt too furiously angry to be afraid, but then, suddenly, as he secured both her hands in one of his and ran his free one experimentally over her body, she froze, all her feminine instincts and fears awakened.

'Keep still,' Ran warned his quarry abruptly. It had come as a shock to discover that she was female. He had assumed that the attempted theft of the car was being carried out by a young boy.

As she heard and recognised Ran's voice, Sylvie's fear immediately changed to a mixture of relief and fury.

'Let go of me,' she demanded immediately.

'Sylvie…?' Ran stared at her in disbelief. 'What the hell…?'

He had relaxed his grip on her hands but his weight was still holding her pinned to the ground and Sylvie wriggled protestingly beneath him, complaining.

'Sylvie,' Ran repeated, still obviously shocked by her presence. 'I thought… I heard the peafowl and thought someone was… I thought you were trying to steal the car… I couldn't tell who you were in the dark,' Ran told her curtly as he read the disbelief in her eyes, her expression revealed to him as the moon grew in strength now that the dusk had given way to proper darkness.

'What are you doing here anyway?' he demanded sharply.

'I needed some fresh air; the windows in my room won't open and I…I decided I might as well walk over here and collect my car… And what about you? I thought *you* were supposed to be going on a date, not creeping around frightening people to death,' Sylvie accused him angrily.

She was becoming acutely and very uncomfortably conscious of the way he was lying on top of her, her legs still entangled with his from when she had tried to escape from him, but now…

Sylvie drew a sharp self-admonitory breath at the direction her thoughts were taking. It was becoming increasingly difficult for her to breathe and not just because of Ran's weight on top of her. She was all too aware of how, when she did breathe, her breasts were pressing against his chest and even more dangerously conscious of the way her pelvis was accommodating itself to the shape of him. She could smell the warm summer night air on his skin and with it the much, much more intimate musky male scent that was him. Somehow or other during their struggle her T-shirt had become separated from her jeans and she was hideously aware that it was too late to regret now the fact that in redressing herself she had not bothered to put back on the sensible white bra she had discarded when she had gone to bed. Instinctively her free hand went to her body to check just how far up her T-shirt had ridden.

'What is it?' Ran asked her, his attention caught by the movement of her hand.

'You're heavy, Ran, you're *hurting* me,' Sylvie told him, not entirely truthfully, as she tried to bury herself in the night's cloaking shadows, but it was too late and she could see from the sudden narrowing of his gaze as it followed the action of her hand that he realised, as she had just done herself, that her wretched T-shirt had ridden up far enough to expose the lower curve of her breasts.

The last thing, the very last thing she wanted was for Ran to study her body in any way at all, so why...why, the moment his gaze fell to her breasts, did they suddenly decide to react to his presence by swelling and firming, her nipples sensually flaunting peaks of explicit womanhood?

'You're not wearing a bra...'

'Thank you, Ran, but I *am* already aware of that fact,' Sylvie snapped at him through gritted teeth, her face hot with colour as she tried to reach the edge of her T-shirt to tug it down. But before she could do so Ran forestalled her, his own fingers curling round the thin white fabric.

Sylvie was in no doubt that Ran *did* intend to pull it down to cover her breasts. She could read his intentions quite plainly in his eyes. So how on earth what happened next *did* happen she was at a complete loss to know.

She moved, and so did Ran's hand. Sylvie froze tensely as she felt his knuckles brush the underside of her breasts; immediately she made an awkward lunging movement away from his touch, forgetting that Ran had hold of the edge of her T-shirt. As she moved Ran tugged and then Sylvie tugged back and Ran let go.

Sylvie wasn't sure which of them it was that made the small hissing sound, expelling their breath as her T-shirt, Lycra added to the cotton to ensure its smooth neat fit, reacted automatically to their tugging action and shot upwards, fully exposing her naked breasts.

Sylvie heard Ran curse and then saw him go very still; motionless herself, Sylvie waited. The sensation of Ran's hand gently cupping her naked breast made her close her eyes in self-defence as she tried to stem the rapture that flooded through her. It wasn't just *what* he was doing, it was the fact that she had once longed for him to touch her, to hold her like this so very, very much, and it was as though all that long-ago feeling and all that long-ago need had suddenly risen up inside her.

'Ran...' She heard herself whisper his name, but the hands she put out to him were there to hold him, not to push him away, and as she felt him lower himself slowly against her again the shudder that ran through her was one of desire and not rejection.

Very slowly and gently his fingertips stroked her breasts, shaping them, exploring them. The night air felt velvet soft and sensual against them but nowhere near as soft nor as sensual as Ran's hands.

Carefully he caressed her and she could see the fierce gleam in his eyes as he looked briefly into hers and then he was bending his head towards her, kissing her with a fierce, passionate intensity that left her totally defenceless. Helplessly she opened her mouth to the hungry demand of his, making a tiny soft keening sound deep in her throat as she responded and matched his passion.

There was something earthy, primitive, inevitable and unstoppable about what was happening. A soft breeze whispered through the trees bordering the gravel and hypersensitively Sylvie heard it, felt its warmth against her skin. The rough cloth of Ran's shirt teased her breasts, making her ache for the feel of his hands against them again. His hands...his mouth... She heard him groan, his fingers biting into her skin as he drew her close, so close that she could feel the hard, aroused pulse of his body. Instinctively her own rose up as though seeking even closer contact with him. His mouth burned hotly

against her throat as he kissed it, his head moving lower
and lower still until she could feel its demanding heat
against her breast.

Sylvie whispered in need, arching up towards him,
almost sobbing in relief as his mouth finally closed over
her nipple, caressing it gently, his tongue laving it and
then flicking erotically against it before he started to
suck on it with a rhythmic urgency that echoed the pulsing heat of his arousal.

Once, long ago, she had dreamt of Ran wanting her
like this, *needing* her like this, all aching, fierce, demanding male passion. Tiny shock waves of desire were
flooding sensuously through her, she wanted him so
badly; eagerly she drew him closer and then froze as
somewhere in the woods a fox screamed noisily to the
moon.

Ran too tensed, lifting his mouth from her body as he
turned his head in the direction of the noise.

Suddenly, abruptly, protected no longer by the heat of
his passion nor the warmth of his body, Sylvie realised
what she was doing. The gravel of the drive which previously she had not even noticed pressed sharply into
her skin, and her face flushed with mortification as she
realised how she must look, how she must *seem* to Ran,
so pathetically eager for his kisses, for *him*, that she...

'Don't touch me,' she warned him shakily as she
yanked down her top and struggled to her feet. 'I feel
sorry for your...for Vicky...if all it takes to make you
unfaithful to her is...'

'You?' Ran supplied tersely for her.

Sylvie's flush deepened, pain filling her body as she
turned away from him so that he wouldn't see how much
he was hurting her.

'We both know that what just happened had nothing to do with... That it wasn't *me*... I could have been *anyone*. My body could have been *anyone's*. You were...'

'So turned on by the sight of your semi-naked breasts that I couldn't resist seeing if they felt and tasted as good as they looked,' Ran told her softly. 'You forget, Sylvie... I've seen them before, and not just seen them but—'

'Stop it, stop it,' Sylvie begged him, instinctively placing her hands over her ears to blot out the sound of his taunting words. That was the last thing she wanted to be reminded about now...the very last... Tears blurred her vision. Frantically she blinked them away; she wasn't going to let Ran see her crying... No way...

Shakily she made her way towards the Discovery whilst Ran watched her broodingly. What the hell could he say to her? She had every right to be furiously angry with him. That gibe about Vicky had been uncalled for, though. Vicky wasn't his love...he didn't *have* a love... There was no relationship, no commitment in his life...unlike her.

Did she respond to Lloyd the same way she had to him, with that aching, intoxicating blend of female need and almost out-of-control hunger?

Ran closed his eyes as he heard Sylvie start the engine of her car.

He had made his fair share of mistakes in his life and had his due portion of regrets, but there was nothing he regretted more than... He swallowed and looked out into the darkness. He hadn't needed what had happened tonight to tell him that there was unfinished business between him and Sylvie.

As he started to walk towards where he had left his car the fierce male ache in his body made him clench his teeth. Right now there was nothing, *nothing*, he wanted more than to finish what they had started. Nothing he wanted more and no one he could have less.

Sylvie's body might still be responsive to him, but Sylvie herself hated him. He knew that. She had told him so often enough.

'Wayne's the man I love,' she had said, throwing the words at him like weapons, and he, too furious, too jealous to respond, had simply walked away without explaining to her that she was a wealthy man's daughter and he might have nothing, but at least, unlike her precious Wayne, he genuinely cared about her, hadn't just been using her!

He had spent the next two days searching Oxford from top to bottom for her, but by then it was too late—she had disappeared. The next time he had seen her she had been with the band of New Age travellers who had invaded Alex's land, quite plainly enjoying flaunting her relationship with its leader in front of him.

'What's wrong?' she had taunted him. '*You* didn't want me...you told me so and you were right, Ran, you're not the one for me...not very much of a man at all compared with Wayne,' she had purred with a sensuously knowing look that had made him feel as if someone was ripping out his guts.

'She and Wayne seem to be lovers,' Alex had confided to him unhappily, and now another man had taken over that role in her life, that *place* in her bed, and he had no right...

Helplessly he stared at the stars. Why the hell had he done it, given in to the temptation to resurrect for himself all the old ghosts, all the old pain? Hadn't he already spent enough nights lying alone in his bed, aching for her, wanting her?

Perhaps Alex was right; perhaps it was time that he looked around for a woman to settle down with, and perhaps once this business was finished and Sylvie was finally out of his life that was exactly what he would do... Perhaps...

CHAPTER FIVE

SYLVIE frowned as she started to double-check what she had just been reading. In a detailed account for the work involved in treating both the wet and dry rot to Haverton Hall, she had only just noticed that slipped in at the back was an additional sheet reporting on some dry rot infestation in the Rectory, Ran's private property, and with it was a brief note confirming that the work on the Rectory would be put in hand before the contractors started working on Haverton Hall itself.

Sylvie could feel her heart starting to thump heavily with a mixture of anger and pain as she re-read the sheet. It wasn't unknown for the owners of the properties the Trust took over to try to drive as hard a bargain as they possibly could. It had fallen to Sylvie on more than one occasion to tactfully inform very grand personages that odd pieces of furniture they had listed as antiques had turned out, on further inspection, to be in fact extremely good copies and therefore not worth the value which had originally been attributed to them. On such occasions a very large supply of tact plus an even larger helping of erring on the side of generosity was called for, but for some reason the possibility of having caught Ran out in such a way evoked within her such strong and confusing emotions that she had to get up from her makeshift desk in front of her bedroom window to pace her bedroom floor whilst she mentally rehearsed exactly how she was going to confront him with her discovery of what he had done. The sum involved wasn't particularly large—and, had Ran gone about things in a different way, she knew perfectly well that the Trust would probably have large-mindedly and generously offered to bear the cost of the work on the Rectory. It was the fact that he had tried to *cheat* them…to deceive and trick her…that Sylvie found so unacceptable, the fact that he probably thought he *had* deceived her, the fact that he was probably secretly laughing at her behind her back. Well, he wasn't going to be laughing when she confronted him, she decided angrily.

A knock on her bedroom door stopped her in her tracks, her body tensing as she called out tersely, 'Come in,' whilst mentally deciding how to mount her attack. But when the door opened it wasn't Ran who walked into her room but the housekeeper, Mrs Elliott.

'Oh, Mrs Elliott,' Sylvie faltered.

'Ran asked me to check with you what you would like for dinner this evening,' the woman told her. 'He landed a fine wild salmon this morning and he said it was a particular favourite of yours…'

Sylvie closed her eyes.

Damn Ran. What was he trying to do to her reminding her, of things, of a past, she would much rather forget?

'That's very kind of you, Mrs Elliott,' she told the other woman crisply, 'but I shall be eating out this evening.'

Previously she had not given the least thought to where she might eat her evening meal, and she knew that her behaviour in refusing Ran's salmon was both illogical and slightly childish, but she hadn't been able to help herself.

Where was Ran anyway…strategically keeping out of

her way? Well, he couldn't do that for ever, and she
certainly intended to tell him what she had discovered
and to demand an explanation of his misuse of the
Trust's funds. No doubt he had imagined that he could
slip the bill for the work on his own property through
with the bill for the cost of the work on Haverton Hall
without anyone being any the wiser. Well, he was going
to learn very quickly his error. Which reminded her—
she really ought to go up to the house and have a word
with whoever was in charge of the company he had hired
to deal with the dry rot. Sylvie pursed her lips. By rights
the contract ought to have been put out to tender, but
she had to admit that by acting so promptly and getting
both the report compiled and the work started Ran had
saved her a good deal of groundwork—and enabled
work to be done on the Rectory at the Trust's expense?

Ten minutes later Sylvie was on her way downstairs
when she heard voices in the hallway, and as she
rounded the curve of the staircase she could see Mrs
Elliott talking with a tall, elegant woman in her late
thirties.

'So you'll tell Ran that I called,' she was saying to
Mrs Elliott.

'Yes, I will, Mrs Edwards,' the other woman was responding respectfully.

Thoughtfully and discreetly Sylvie studied her. Tall,
slender, expensively dressed, immaculately made up, she
was the type of woman whom Sylvie could remember
Ran favouring and she immediately guessed that she
must be Ran's current woman-friend. There was certainly that very confident, almost proprietorial air about
her that suggested she was far more than simply a mere
visitor to the house. She turned away from Mrs Elliott

and then saw Sylvie, her expression changing slightly
and becoming, if not challenging then certainly assess-
ing, Sylvie recognised as she continued on her way
downstairs.

'I'm just on my way to Haverton Hall, Mrs Elliott,'
she told Ran's daily calmly, adding with an impetuosity
she later refused to examine or analyse, 'Please thank
Ran for his offer of dinner.'

Out of the corner of her eye she could see the way
Ran's woman-friend's eyes darkened as she watched her,
and she had just reached the front door when Mrs Elliott
stopped her, announcing, 'Oh, I'm so sorry, I almost
forgot; Ran asked me to tell you that if you wanted to
finish going over the big house he'd be back around
three.'

'Did he? That's very thoughtful of him. How very
obliging of him,' Sylvie responded acidly. 'When he
does return, Mrs Elliott, please tell him that there's no
need for him to put himself to so much trouble. I have
my own set of keys to Haverton Hall.'

Without waiting for the older woman to make any
further response, Sylvie pulled open the front door. How
dared he? she fumed as she hurried towards her hire car.
She had no need of either his company or his permission
to view the Hall. Furiously she started the Discovery,
sending up an angry spray of gravel as she reversed and
then headed for the drive.

She was over halfway to Haverton Hall before she felt
calm enough to slow down a little, her face burning as
hotly as her temper. It was not up to Ran to tell her what
she could and could not do—not any longer.

As she brought the Discovery to a halt outside the
house she hastily averted her eyes from the spot where

last night... What had happened last night was something she had no intention of dwelling on nor trying to analyse; it had been a mistake, an error of judgement, a total and complete aberration and something which had, no doubt, been brought on by some kind of jet lag, some kind of inexplicable imbalance, and it really wasn't worthy of having her waste any time agonising over it.

Unlocking the huge door, she turned the handle and took a deep breath as she pushed it open and stepped inside. Resolutely ignoring the echoing sound of her own footsteps, she hurried to where she and Ran had left off their inspection the previous day. In her bag she had an inventory and a plan of the house, but an hour later she was forced to admit that it was proving far less interesting inspecting the rooms on her own than it had been yesterday, with Ran's informative descriptions of the rooms and their original uses.

From previous experience she knew that in a very short space of time she herself would be completely familiar with the house's layout and its history, but right now... She gave a small scream as a mouse scuttled across the floor right in front of her. She had always had an irrational fear of them—they moved so fast and so far, and she had never totally got over an unpleasant childhood experience of having one jump towards her as it ran from one of the stable cats.

She was working her way along the upper floor when she suddenly heard Ran calling her name. Stiffening, she stood where she was. Mrs Elliott must have told him that he would find her here. In her bag she had the report and the costings he had commissioned for treatment of the wet and dry rot. Firmly she walked towards the door, opened it and called out, 'I'm up here, Ran...'

'You shouldn't have come here on your own,' he cautioned her as he came down the corridor towards her.

'Why not? The house isn't haunted, is it?' she mocked him sarcastically.

'Not as far as I know,' he agreed, 'but the floors, especially on these upper two floors, aren't totally to be trusted, and if you should have had an accident—'

'How very thoughtful of you to be concerned, Ran,' Sylvie interrupted him. 'Almost as thoughtful as it was of you to commission these reports.'

As she spoke she removed the reports from her bag and waved them under his nose. 'Or am I being naive and would ''self-interested'' be a much truer description?'

Ran started to frown.

'I don't know what you're trying to imply, Sylvie,' he began, but she wouldn't let him go any further, challenging him immediately,

'Don't you, Ran? I read the reports from the surveyors this morning. Tucked in at the back of the estimates you'd obtained was this...'

Coolly she handed him the costing for the work on the Rectory.

'So?' Ran shrugged after he had scanned the piece of paper she proffered.

'This particular costing relates to work that needs to be carried out on the *Rectory*, your *own private* house,' Sylvie pointed out patiently.

'And...?' Ran demanded, frowning at her before telling her, 'I'm sorry, Sylvie, but I'm afraid I'm at a loss to understand exactly what it is you're driving at. The Rectory needed some work doing on it to put right the dry rot the surveyors found, and—'

'You decided to slip the bill for that work in amongst the bills for the work that was needed on Haverton Hall, to *lose* it amongst the admittedly far greater cost of the work needed here!'

'What?' Ran demanded ominously quietly, his expression as well as his voice betraying his outrage.

'I don't like what you're trying to suggest, Sylvie,' he told her sharply.

She shook her head and told him thinly, 'Neither do I, Ran. But the facts speak for themselves.'

'Do they?' His mouth twisted bitterly. 'I rather think it's your overheated imagination that's doing the "speaking" through your totally erroneous interpretation of them,' he told her through gritted teeth.

'You can't deny the evidence of this report,' Sylvie reminded him sternly.

'What evidence?' Ran demanded. 'This is a report and an estimate for work on the Rectory—work which I have had carried out at *my own* expense; the only reason the report and costing is there at all is because I omitted to remove it when I had the documents copied for you...'

'*You've* paid for the work on the Rectory yourself?' Sylvie queried in disbelief.

Ran's mouth thinned.

'Perhaps you'd like to see the receipts,' he challenged her.

'Yes, I would,' Sylvie responded doggedly, refusing to let him cow her even though she could feel her face starting to burn self-consciously and her stomach beginning to churn as she contemplated just how foolish she was going to look if Ran did produce such receipts.

'Mrs Elliott tells me that you're going out for dinner this evening.'

Sylvie stared at him, thrown by his abrupt change of subject.

'Yes. Yes, I am,' she agreed.

'There isn't a decent restaurant for miles,' he told her, 'and certainly not one that offers fresh wild salmon; it's always been one of your favourites...'

'Perhaps my tastes have changed,' Sylvie said a little loftily, adding robustly, 'Unlike yours...'

As he started to frown she explained sweetly, 'I saw your...*friend*. She called at the Rectory just as I was leaving. I'm sure she'd be more than delighted to share your salmon with you, Ran,' she told him coolly. 'Now, about those receipts...'

Inwardly Sylvie shivered a bit as she saw the anger flare in his eyes but outwardly she stood her ground. It was, after all, her job to make sure that the Trust wasn't cheated—by *anyone*.

'Of course,' Ran told her formally, inclining his head as though in defeat, but then, just as Sylvie started to draw a relieved breath, he gave her a dangerously vulpine smile and told her softly, 'But I'm afraid it will have to be this evening as I have a business meeting tomorrow morning and then I shall probably be away for several days...'

'With your...friend...?'

Later Sylvie could only despair over whatever it was that had led her to make such a dangerously betraying and provocative remark, but inexplicably the words were out before she could stop them, causing Ran, who had been on the point of turning away from her, to turn back and slowly scrutinise her from head to foot before asking her softly, 'If you mean Vicky, is that really any of your business...*or* the Trust's...?'

He had caught her out and Sylvie knew it. It most certainly was not part of her duty as the Trust's representative to ask any questions about his personal life, and she was mortified that she had done so.

'If you want to see the receipts for the work on the Rectory then it will have to be this evening, Sylvie,' Ran was repeating briskly. 'Shall we say about eight-thirty?'

Before she could say anything else he had gone, striding across the dusty floor and leaving her to watch his departing back.

It was a good ten minutes after she had heard the noise of his Land Rover engine die away before Sylvie felt able to continue with her work. Her intelligence told her that their antagonism was coming between her and the normally wisely efficient way in which she dealt with even the most awkward of the Trust's clients, but her emotions refused to allow her to back down, to climb down. If she was wary of him, suspicious of him, then she had every right to be.

And every right to as good as accuse him of trying to defraud the Trust?

She started to nibble anxiously at her bottom lip. If she was wrong about him trying to get the Trust to cover the cost of work he had had done on his own home, and if he chose to complain to Lloyd—

Irritably Sylvie reminded herself why she was here.

Although the house wasn't any larger than others she had dealt with, it certainly seemed to possess far more small interconnecting rooms here on its upper storeys. She rubbed the dust from the window of one of them and peered out at the countryside spread all around her. From here she could see the river where Ran must have caught his fish. It wound lazily in a long half-loop through the parkland which surrounded the house. Although the terrain here in Derbyshire was very different from that which surrounded Alex's home, it was disturbingly easy, looking down towards the river, to remember the many happy hours she had spent with Alex and Ran as a young girl, watching them as they worked together, helping them fish and later learning from them their countryside skills.

One of the ways in which, hopefully, ultimately, Haverton Hall could generate its own income would be, as Ran had suggested in the initial approach he had made to the Trust, for the house to be let out to large corporations and groups along with its fishing and shooting rights. The Trust adopted a policy that no game existing on its lands could be killed simply for sport—a very strict culling programme was put in place where necessary and the art of tracking animals was taught as a skill for its own sake rather than with a view to killing. That had been a condition which she herself had insisted on persuading the trustees to adopt, and it made her stop and frown slightly to herself now as she was forced to remember how it had been Ran who had first shown her that it was not necessary to kill to enjoy such traditional country sports.

Ran...

Sylvie was still thinking about him some time later when an exhausting drive through the virtually uninhabited countryside which surrounded the house had only produced three small villages, not one of which boasted a restaurant.

In the small pub in the third village the landlord shook his head when she asked about food and apologised.

'We don't have the trade for it round here, although I could perhaps see if there's any sandwiches left over from lunchtime.'

Smiling wanly, Sylvie shook her head. She was hungry, very hungry in fact, and had been looking forward to sitting down to a proper hot meal.

'There's a good place over Lintwell way,' the pub manager was continuing helpfully, 'but that's a good twenty-five miles from here.'

Twenty-five miles. Sylvie's stomach was already starting to rumble. Against her will she had a mental vision of Ran's salmon, pink and poached, served with delicious home-grown baby new potatoes and fresh vegetables and, of course, a proper hollandaise sauce. Her mouth watered.

It was gone seven o'clock now, though, and if she were to drive to Lintwell and back and eat as well that would mean she would be late for her meeting with Ran and there was no way she was going to allow him the opportunity to accuse her of being unprofessional.

Refusing the landlord's offer of the afternoon's left-over sandwiches, she made her way back to her car. She would just have to go without a meal tonight, she told herself firmly; after all, it wouldn't be the end of the world. She was hardly going to starve... But oh, that salmon and... Ran was quite right. It was her favourite.

It was almost eight when Sylvie pulled up outside the Rectory's front door.

Her earlier hunger had turned into a gnawing irritation that was making her head ache and her temper on edge.

Low blood sugar, she told herself sternly. All you need is a sweet drink.

All she *needed* maybe, but not all she wanted. What she wanted…

What on earth was the matter with her? she derided herself as she opened the front door. Other women her age daydreamed and fantasised about having men, not meals.

Eight o'clock. She just had time to get showered and changed before her meeting with Ran. She wanted to run through her figures again, but if, as he said, he had paid for the work himself and he had the receipts to prove it… Perhaps she *had* been too quick to accuse him…

'Sylvie…'

She froze at the bottom of the stairs as she heard Ran's voice. When she turned her head he was standing in an open doorway several feet away from her.

'Mrs Elliott is going to serve dinner at eight-thirty so you've got half an hour to get ready…'

A dozen questions and just as many denials and arguments sprang immediately to Sylvie's lips, but somehow she managed not to utter them and she was at the top of the stairs before she managed to ask herself why she had not simply told Ran that she had eaten already.

Why? The audible rumble of her stomach as she opened her bedroom door gave its own answer. Even so, it galled her to know that Ran had guessed she would have to return to the house without having found somewhere to eat. But just let him try to make something of it, Sylvie decided fiercely as, having had her shower, she changed into a long silky black jersey dress, brushing her hair and quickly re-doing her make-up before check-ing the time.

Almost eight-thirty. Taking a deep breath, Sylvie checked her appearance in the mirror and then, holding her head high, headed for the bedroom door.

Her jersey dress, plain black and unadorned, might not, to anyone but the *cognoscente*, reveal the fact that it had cost her the best part of a month's wages and carried the label of one of New York's top designers—the uninitiated might be deceived by the simple design and the way the heavy fabric discreetly hinted at rather than clung more obviously to Sylvie's slender figure. But even the most self-confessed sartorial ignoramus would have reacted to the way Ran looked when Sylvie saw him waiting for her at the bottom of the stairs.

Used as she was to seeing him wearing casual work clothes, and perhaps because that was the image she held engraved in her mind's eye—jeans fitting snugly against the hard muscle of his thighs, checked work shirt rolled up at the sleeves and just open enough at the neck to reveal the silky dark expanse of body hair which so temptingly and tormentingly made one's fingers long to unfasten a few more buttons and explore just how thick, just how silky that soft dark hair actually was—Sylvie had forgotten how very male Ran could look in formal clothes.

And although he hadn't gone so far as to change into a dinner suit he *was* wearing a pair of well-cut dark trousers and a crisp white shirt.

The fact that he was just shrugging on his jacket as she came down the stairs afforded Sylvie an unwanted glimpse of the lethal maleness of the muscles in his torso and made her hesitate betrayingly just for a second before continuing her journey downwards.

He had changed his clothes simply to have dinner with her.

Why? Because he knew very well the effect his appearance would have on any susceptible woman and because he intended to use that fact to distract her, confuse her when she needed all her attention, all her concentration to ascertain the truth about that invoice? Or was she letting her imagination run away with her? Was the woman he had dressed so elegantly for not her but—?

Was he perhaps seeing the other woman after their meeting had finished?

'We've just got time for a drink before dinner if you'd like one,' Ran told her calmly, but his glance, Sylvie was sure, had rested for just a betraying fraction of a second on the soft thrust of her breasts before it had lifted to her face. Her heart started to thump giddily.

'No… No drink, thanks,' she refused, giving him a thin smile as she added deliberately, 'I generally find that alcohol and business don't mix.'

Giving a small shrug, Ran opened the dining-room door for her and waited for her to precede him inside. As she did so, Sylvie caught the clean, sharp scent of his freshly showered body and the giddying thump of her vulnerable heart became a frighteningly heavy ache.

'I…I've brought the estimates down with me,' she told him quickly, lifting the papers she was holding in front of him, but Ran shook his head.

'After dinner,' he told her dismissively, adding, '*I* generally find that good food and poor communication don't mix.'

Poor communication. Sylvie gave him a fulminating look before taking the chair he had pulled out for her.

The salmon was every bit as delicious as Sylvie had imagined and so, too, was the home-made summer pudding served with fresh cream that followed it. The cheese they ate to finish the meal was made locally, Ran informed her, adding that he had been wondering if he might not produce something similar himself, but that he had decided the costs involved were prohibitive.

To have dinner alone with Ran like this would once have made her feel so excited, so...so thrilled because she had been so besottedly in love with him. Of course, she would hardly have been able to do justice to the meal because then her fevered imagination would have been thrilling her with images of the two of them together alone, after dinner, Ran taking her in his arms and...

'I've asked Mrs Elliott to serve coffee in the library...'

The crisp, businesslike tone of Ran's voice cut across her treacherous thoughts. Guiltily, Sylvie pushed them away, reminding herself severely of just why she was here.

'Here is the separate estimate I asked for, for the work which needed doing here, and here is the receipt I obtained for that work.'

Her facial muscles rigid, Sylvie willed her hand not to tremble betrayingly as she took the papers from Ran and then looked at them. She was furious with herself for giving him the opportunity to put her in the wrong.

Her eyes strayed to the date at the top of the receipted

invoice. She wasn't going to give in yet. Standing up, she handed the papers back to Ran and told him dismissively, 'What I can see is a signed and dated receipt, Ran.'

'Showing that the invoice was settled several weeks ago…'

'*Purporting* to show that it was settled several weeks ago,' Sylvie pointed out stubbornly. 'For all I know this date could have been written on the invoice last week…or…' She paused meaningfully before adding with a triumphant smile, 'Or even today…'

She had started to walk away when Ran stopped her, grabbing hold of her arm and swinging her round to face him as he exploded, 'Are you *really* trying to accuse me of falsifying this receipt? For God's sake, Sylvie, what the hell kind of man do you think I am?'

Pointedly Sylvie ignored his question and stared down at where he was still holding onto her arm instead as she demanded icily, 'Let go of me, Ran.'

'Let *go* of you…? Do you realise what you're saying, what you're *accusing* me of doing? You're not a teenager any more, Sylvie, and if this is some kind of petty attempt to—'

'No, I'm not.' Sylvie interrupted him furiously. 'I'm the Trust's representative here at Haverton and as such it's my job to protect the Trust's interests and its investments… If I think that someone, *anyone*, is trying to cheat the Trust or misuse its funds, then it's my job to—'

'Your *job*…?' Ran laughed savagely. 'You sound very high-minded for someone who's slept her way into her ''job'' via her boss's bed.'

There was a second's pause and then a white heat, a zigzag of pure fury and frustrated womanly pride, hit

Sylvie like a bolt of lightning. Immediately she reacted in the only way her outraged female instincts knew, lifting her hand and slapping Ran's face in furious rejection of his insult.

Sylvie didn't know which of them was the more shocked—she who had delivered the blow or Ran who had received it. For a single beat of time they both stood completely still, staring at one another. Sylvie could feel her heart racing, she could see the white, slowly reddening imprint of her hand against Ran's dark skin and she could see too the vengeful male fury darkening his eyes. Too late to regret her behaviour, or to turn and run; Ran was still holding onto her arm, and as she tried to pull away he dragged her towards him, his eyes glittering with fevered rage.

Sylvie knew, even before it happened, just what he was going to do. She was already closing her eyes and whispering helplessly, 'No,' as she felt the hard, bruising pressure of his mouth against her own.

To be kissed like this, in fury, in punishment, and with a blind, searing male desire to dominate, was something totally outside all her experience. Her body had no defences against it, no knowledge of how to deal with it. Panic and anger surged through her body. She was no helpless Victorian virgin, she was a modern woman, able to give as good as she got. Fiercely she returned the anger of Ran's furious kiss. He was already prising apart her closed lips with his tongue, demanding entry to the intimacy of her mouth, not with the tender touch of a lover but with the forceful pressure of a warrior, a victor. Wildly Sylvie tried to evade him, but he was holding onto her too strongly and all her attempts to break free did was to bring her body into even closer contact with his. She still fought to break free, pummelling his chest with her fists and then, when that did no good and there was no longer any space between their bodies for her to do so, angrily raking her nails down his back.

Somewhere, deep down, in the murkiest of murky waters of her subconscious, lay the knowledge that this wasn't just about the insult he had given her, nor her angry reaction to it; that this explosion of furious emotion this need to reach out and hurt him, to damage and destroy what was left of the love she had once felt for him, had its roots, its being, in something very, very different from mere insulted female pride.

'Little vixen,' she heard Ran muttering thickly against her mouth as he caught hold of her hand. 'Your elderly lover might need the stimulus of having his back scratched raw when you make love but I certainly don't.'

Shocked into awareness of what she was doing by his words, Sylvie went still.

Lloyd might not be her lover, but that didn't really matter; it was the impact of what Ran had just said to her that hurt and wounded so badly, the fact that he was comparing the anger and mutual hatred they were both expressing with an act that, to Sylvie, was one which should be highlighted and hallmarked with tenderness and true emotional love. Suddenly all the anger drained out of her. She felt sickened, not just by Ran's words but more importantly by what she herself had done. A vixen, Ran had called her, but when animals mated they did so for a specific purpose; their coming together was never an act of cruelty or cynical disregard for everything that sharing the intimacy of one's body with another should be.

Sylvie could feel her eyes starting to fill with tears.

Ran had pulled back from her to look at her, and, taking advantage of his slackened grip, she pulled herself free of him and started to walk quickly, if a little unsteadily, towards the library door.

Startled, Ran called out to her, following her out into the hallway, watching as she disappeared up the stairs. Should he go after her, apologise, explain...? That look he had just seen in her eyes had shocked him. It was more the look of a hurt child than a mature, experienced, worldly woman, and besides... There had been no call for him to make that remark to her about Lloyd. Her relationship with the other man was, after all, her own affair, even if he... God... For a moment there the feeling, the sharp dig of her nails into his skin through the fabric of his shirt, had made him ache so badly for the feel of her naked body beneath his own, the feel, the scent, the taste of her. And if he could have his time again... But what was the point in thinking about, *reliving* old memories, old mistakes?

He had done what he had thought was best at the time, the honourable thing to do...

CHAPTER SIX

WEARILY Sylvie looked at the luminous face of her watch. Half past one in the morning. She had been awake for the last hour, stubbornly courting sleep, angrily refusing to allow her thoughts to take control, to force her to remember.

She was too hyped up for sleep, too *afraid* to sleep just in case she... She what? Dreamed of Ran?

She looked across at the desk in front of the window. One of the small pleasures of living in the depths of the country was that one did not need to close the curtains at night. There was nothing Sylvie liked more than being able to see the night sky.

When her mother had first married Alex's father and they had gone to live in his ancestral home, she had been overwhelmed at first by the darkness of the huge house. It had been Ran who had guessed her fears and apprehensions after he had found her sleepwalking that night. Ran who had been staying at the house instead of his cottage one weekend, 'babysitting' her in the absence of her mother, and who had taken her, not back to bed, but to his own room where he had made her a hot drink and talked to her, showing her the telescope he used to watch the night sky.

The binoculars beside it he had used for another, more mundane purpose. As the estate manager one of his jobs had been to keep a sharp look-out for poachers. The night had no fears for Ran, and through him she too had learned to appreciate its special beauties. It had been Ran who had taken her to watch the badger cubs at play, earning her mother's anger. Sylvie quickly stopped that line of thought. Since she couldn't sleep she might as well try to do some work; that at least would be a far more profitable way of spending her time than thinking about Ran.

Her mouth still felt slightly swollen and sensitive from the way he had kissed her earlier. Her face started to burn as she recalled again the comment he had made to her about her being a vixen—and about Lloyd being her lover.

What would he say if he knew that she had only had one lover and that lover had been a man who hadn't really wanted her, a man she had had to coax and beg to take her to bed, a man who had told her that he felt no love for her, that what had happened between them had been a mistake, an error of judgement best forgotten?

No. No. No. Angrily, Sylvie buried her face in her hands, but it was too late; there was no pushing back the memories now, they were here, surrounding her, flooding out any kind of denial or rational thought.

She had been at university by then; had, in fact, gone there unwillingly. So intense and all-consuming had been the ferocity of her teenage love for Ran, so burningly immediate and sharp-fanged her desire for him, that she had not been able to bear the thought of putting any kind of distance between them. Every spare minute she had, every excuse she could use, she *had* used—to be with Ran. As Alex's stepsister it had been easy enough for her to spend her free time at the estate, joining the group of local teenagers who were helping Ran with some of his environmental projects had given her even more opportunity to be with him. Not that Ran himself had seemed to be aware of her feelings, even though she had done everything she could to show him how she felt.

There had been that afternoon she had fallen into the muddy lake they had been cleaning. Ran had pulled her out, grinning at her mud-covered clothes and hair.

'I need a bath,' she had complained, grimacing.

'A *bath*?' Ran had laughed. 'There's no way Alex's housekeeper is going to let you into the house like that. I'd better take you back to the cottage with me and hose you down outside before I let you go back, otherwise we'll both be in real trouble.'

His cottage... How she had trembled at the thought, imagining not the prosaic cleaning-up operation Ran had so teasingly referred to but something far more intimate, her body soaking in a tub of blissfully hot water whilst Ran lovingly soaped her clean...

'What's wrong?' he had asked her, frowning at her. 'You've gone very red. Are you feeling ill?'

Ill... Sick with love, with *longing* for him, would have been the appropriate answer, but she had been too naive, too shy to make it. Instead she had shaken her head and dutifully climbed into his battered Land Rover for the drive back to his small estate cottage.

The sensual intimacy she had so dangerously imagined had proved to be just that—a fantasy.

Ran had made her remove her clothes in his small back porch, sternly admonishing her not to move off the old towel he had put down on the floor and to give him a shout once she was undressed and wrapped in the towel he had left her.

'I'll put your stuff in the washer—Alex's housekeeper will kill me if she sees it—and then you can have a quick shower upstairs. You'll have to go home in my stuff but at least it will be clean.'

'These towels are awfully thin,' she had remarked critically once she was standing wrapped in the protection of the largest of them, and Ran had returned to scoop up her filthy clothes.

'Mmm... I use them to dry the dogs,' Ran had told her unromantically, grinning at her when he saw her expression. 'They're the ones who should be pulling a face,' he said. 'When *they* come back covered in mud they get hosed down outside before they're even allowed in.'

'I'm not a dog, I'm a...' A woman, she had been about to say, but then she had stopped as Ran had stooped to pick up her white briefs from the stone floor, her face turning an unsophisticated shade of pink when she saw how small they looked held in his strongly masculine hand.

The wet had seeped right through her jeans to her briefs, but Ran's eyebrows had risen as he'd studied them and then her.

'It's all right... I can go home without them; it won't matter under...my...your jeans,' Sylvie had told him helpfully, far too innocent and young then to understand just how sensuously provocative it could be for a woman to go naked beneath her clothes—and even more so when the clothes, the *jeans* she was wearing, were his and not her own.

'It's okay; I think I've got something you can wear,' Ran had told her laconically.

She had been young and naive but not so young nor

so naive as not to be able to guess where the tiny pretty lacy briefs Ran had given her might have come from, and the knowledge that they must have belonged to another woman had cast a shadow not just over the whole day, but over everything.

She had once heard Alex joking with Ran about his taste for older women.

'I'm not in the market for commitment or marriage,' Ran had returned. 'But I'm not about to turn myself into a monk either,' he had admitted frankly. Neither of them had known that she was listening as she hesitated outside Alex's library door on her way past.

'So a woman who knows what life's all about, who's been married and decided that it isn't for her, suits me fine.'

She hadn't been able to hide her massive crush on Ran before she'd left for university, in fact had openly offered her love to him, but he had determinedly pushed it away—just as he had also determinedly pushed her away.

She had noticed it again at Alex's annual Christmas party. Her mother had been there, turning her nose up at such little country pursuits, but Sylvie hadn't cared. She'd been determined that Ran was going to dance with her and that she was going to claim a Christmas kiss from him.

She had been wearing a new dress and high heels. She had put her hair up and worn make-up. Alex had looked at her with tender amusement when she had come downstairs, but there had been no tenderness in Ran's eyes later that evening when he had removed her arms from around his neck, refusing to give her the kiss she had begged him for. It had taken three glasses of wine before she had had the courage to approach him and, horrendously, she could feel her eyes starting to fill with tears as he'd unlocked her arms from around his neck and started to turn away from her.

'Ran, please…' she had pleaded, but he had ignored her, stony-faced and blank-eyed, as he'd walked away from her.

And, as though that hadn't been bad enough, to compound the evening's heartache and humiliation, she had seen him less than an hour later dancing with the newly divorced wife of one of Alex's tenants, holding her tightly against his body as he caressed her under the dim lights, bending his head to kiss her with heart-shaking passion before leading her outside.

She had been so jealous, so burned up with pain that even her skin had felt raw and tender.

Later, naively, she'd told herself that Ran hadn't meant to hurt her, that he probably still thought of her as a child and not a woman, and so she had gone on clinging to her self-created delusions.

All through her first year at university, as much as she had wanted to hate Ran, she had also yearned for him, dreaming of him, longing for him, promising herself that one day it would be different, one day he would look at her and love her.

She had refused dates from the boys she met on her courses and only attended the regulation student parties because the other girls had teased her into it. Naturally gregarious, although no one could ever come to mean to her what Ran meant, she had nevertheless made several platonic friendships with various boys she had met at university. One of them she had particularly taken to; shy and self-effacing, David had only come to university because of family pressure. As the youngest of his family he'd been expected to follow in the footsteps of his elder sisters and brothers, all of whom had graduated with honours.

'What did you really want to do?' Sylvie had asked him.

'Paint,' he had told her simply.

Sylvie's discovery that he was taking drugs had saddened but not particularly shocked her. They were, after all, a feature of university life, although she herself had stayed clear of them.

It had been David who had persuaded her to attend the rave party where he had introduced her to Wayne. She had guessed that Wayne was his supplier but had naively assumed then that Wayne was no more than a generous-minded individual who had the contacts to supply his friends with drugs, and that it was they who pressured him into obtaining them for them rather than the other way around. Without directly saying so, Wayne had implied that they were two of a kind, individuals who stood out from the crowd. His street-wise sophistication had reminded her in some odd way of Ran. Perhaps because, like Ran, Wayne was older than her and the friends she'd mixed with. She had listened half enviously when he had told her of his plans to spend the summer with a group of eco-warriors, travelling the country.

Sylvie had always been idealistic, and Wayne's description of the way the group were dedicated to preventing the destruction of the countryside by greedy power barons had increased her sense of comradeship with him and with the group he was joining.

Just as importantly, Wayne had seemed to understand

the problems she was having in convincing her mother that she was now an adult.

'She's such a snob,' she had told Wayne ruefully, wrinkling her nose.

'She wouldn't much approve of me, then,' he had countered, and although she had shaken her head Sylvie had been forced to admit that he was right. She had confided to Wayne how uncomfortable it often made her feel that she should be so privileged. Alex gave her an allowance and her mother was constantly visiting her and fussing over whether or not she was eating properly and wearing the right kind of clothes. Her mother had never wanted her to go to university. She had bemoaned the fact that girls like Sylvie no longer had the opportunity to ''come out'' properly, as she had done as a girl. Alex had been the driving force behind her moving off to university. Time, he said, for her to grow and find out about herself.

It had not been long after her disclosure that she received an allowance that Wayne had asked to borrow money from her. Of course she had given it to him. He was a friend...

And then, after she had given Wayne the money he had asked for, she had discovered that she needed to buy some new course books, and that stupidly she had not realised that she had an advance rent bill due for the small flat she lived in.

She had had to telephone Alex to ask him for an advance on her forthcoming allowance. She had felt uncomfortable about doing so, but after a small pause, when she had stammeringly explained that she had loaned some money to a friend, he had said quietly that she could leave the matter with him.

Naively she had assumed that that meant that he would send her a cheque, and suddenly she'd had more important things to worry about than money. David, her friend, was dead. He had collapsed at a rave party and been rushed into hospital, but it had been too late to save him.

His family had taken him home to bury him and they had also made it plain that they did not want any of his university friends to attend his funeral.

'They blame us for what happened to him,' one of his other friends told Sylvie angrily. 'They're the ones who are at fault. He never wanted to come here…'

Sylvie was too upset to make any comment when Wayne asked for another loan, and he was moody and sharp-tempered with her, mocking her upbringing and taunting her with her naiveté and innocence.

That hurt Sylvie but she said nothing. She knew that he would soon be leaving the city to join the eco-warriors, who were beginning to drift away from the site of their recent defeat over a large motorway extension and to make their way south to meet up with another group, who were trying to persuade the Government to give permission for some land previously owned by the Army to be opened to the general public.

To Sylvie it sounded a good cause.

'Come with us,' Wayne suggested, and then he laughed sneeringly as he added, 'But no, of course you won't… Mummy wouldn't like it, would she?'

Sylvie said nothing. She was still too numbed by David's death. University life, which at first had seemed to promise so much freedom…which she had hoped would be the passage which would carry her effortlessly into womanhood and Ran's love…was proving to be far more painful and difficult than she had envisaged.

She had lost weight and hope, and now her work was beginning to suffer too.

The weather was hot and sticky, with the threat of thunder forever present in the air. They needed a good storm, Sylvie reflected early one evening as she returned to her small flat. She wasn't hungry, and the prospect of an evening spent over her books didn't appeal in the least. She missed David and their discussions and she missed Ran even more.

The day had been so hot and the flat was so airless that she showered in a vain attempt to get cool, pulling over her naked body an old cotton shirt which had once belonged to Alex, too drained and lethargic even to think of getting properly dressed. Half an hour later Wayne arrived, carrying a bottle of wine which he insisted on opening even though she told him that she didn't want anything to drink. In the end it was easier to give in than to argue, but she stood her ground over the drug he offered her, firmly shaking her head.

'Please yourself,' he told her easily, but Sylvie noticed that he didn't have one himself either.

'Any chance of letting me have that money?' he asked her a few minutes later as he lounged on her small sofa, watching her as she tried to work. There was a look in his eyes that made her feel uncomfortable, and not just because she couldn't give him the loan he wanted; no, it was more than that, and suddenly she was acutely conscious of her nudity beneath Alex's shirt.

'I'm sorry, I can't…not at the moment,' she apologised. 'I…I'm waiting for Alex to send me a cheque.

Wayne, I don't want to be a bad host, but really I have to work…'

'You want me to leave…'

'If you don't mind,' Sylvie agreed, waving her hand in the direction of the books she had spread out on the small table in front of her.

For a moment she thought he was going to argue with her, but to her relief he didn't, walking instead towards the door. Eager to see him leave, Sylvie went with him. As she opened the door for him she saw the Land Rover pulling to a halt a little further down the road and her heart started to race with frantic excitement. As though aware of her loss of attention, and angered by it, to her shock Wayne suddenly reached for her, grabbing hold of her and forcing her back against the open door, his mouth hot and wet on hers as he kissed her roughly.

Immediately Sylvie pulled away, but not in time to stop Ran, who was stepping out of the Land Rover and walking towards her, from seeing what had happened, nor from witnessing how she was dressed, she saw uncomfortably as she felt his glance scorch her shirt-clad body.

To her relief Wayne's mobile phone had started to ring and he was already heading for his car, his back towards her as he talked in a low voice into the telephone.

As Ran's long-legged, determined stride brought him closer to her door, Sylvie could only stand and watch.

'Ran!' she exclaimed weakly when he reached her. 'What a surprise. I didn't know… I didn't expect…'

'Obviously not,' was Ran's terse response as he stepped past her and into her small hallway, firmly closing the door behind him as he told her sardonically, 'I'm sorry if my arrival is inopportune, although something tells me that it would have been a lot less opportune had I arrived, say, half an hour ago.'

Sylvie's face flamed as she saw the way he was looking at her and realised what he meant. Ran thought that she and Wayne were lovers.

'It's not...we weren't... Wayne is just a friend...' she finally managed to tell him defensively.

Ran's eyebrows immediately shot up.

'A friend! Tell me, Sylvie, do you normally receive your *friends* wearing just one of their shirts...?'

'This isn't Wayne's shirt; it's one of Alex's old ones,' she protested, hot-faced.

What was Ran doing here? Why had he come to see her? Her heart started to thump frantically.

'Alex's shirt?' Ran was frowning at her as he studied her.

'Yes... I...I like to wear it... It makes me think of home...of Alex and you. I miss you both,' she told him daringly, holding her breath as she waited for his response.

There had to be *some* reason for his being here and his reaction to Wayne's presence... Was she daring to hope too much in thinking that beneath his anger he might *just* be a little jealous? She was a woman now, she reminded herself, not a child, and—

'Home...?' Ran cut across her increasingly buoyant thoughts. 'I doubt your mother would enjoy hearing you describe Otel Place as your home.'

Sylvie bit her lip. It was true that her mother did not approve of her attachment to Otel Place and would have preferred it if, like her, Sylvie had been a city person.

'I'm an adult now,' she told Ran bravely. 'I make my own decisions, my own choices...'

'I see... And entertaining your friends wearing nothing but one of Alex's shirts is one of those choices, is it, Sylvie?'

Her face burned. There was no hint of jealousy in his voice now, only a familiar older-brother note of censure.

'I...I wasn't expecting Wayne to come round. It was so hot. I had a shower and...'

'Wayne... This wouldn't be the friend who's borrowed half your last quarter's allowance from you, would it?' Ran challenged her.

Sylvie blanched. Alex had obviously told him about that; she wished that he hadn't.

'I... He'll pay me back.' She defended both Wayne's request and her own acceptance of it.

'Things have certainly changed since *my* time at university,' Ran told her cynically. 'Then it was the man who did the chasing, the pursuing, not the woman who had to secure the man's attentions by offering him money.'

Sylvie stared at him, unable to keep either her shock or the pain his words had caused her from showing in her eyes.

'It isn't like that... I *haven't* been pursuing Wayne. I don't...'

She stopped abruptly and looked away from him. How could she tell Ran of all men...people...that she didn't run after his sex, when he had good reason to believe otherwise after the ways she had so blatantly revealed her feelings for him? Now he was looking at her in that horribly cynical way, his mouth twisting in mocking contempt.

'Alex asked me to come,' he told her as she remained silent. 'He's had to go away on business but he asked me to come and give you this…'

As he spoke Ran was removing a cheque from his wallet which he handed to her.

Swallowing hard, Sylvie took it from him.

'You could have posted it to me,' she told him in a small voice.

'Alex wanted it delivered in person.'

'It's a long drive… I could… Would you like something to drink…to eat…?'

'Coffee will be fine,' Ran told her shortly, following her as she automatically started to walk into her small living room.

The bottle of wine Wayne had brought with him was still on the table, her own glass nearly empty, and Sylvie saw the hard look Ran gave it as he walked past her work table.

A wooden divider separated the living room end of the room from the small kitchenette, and Ran leaned against it as Sylvie bustled about making them both a cup of coffee.

'You've lost weight,' Ran told her abruptly when she finally handed him his mug. 'It is just sex this friend of yours is dealing in, isn't it, Sylvie…?'

As the meaning of his words sank in Sylvie put down her own mug of coffee, her face burning with indignation.

'I'm not taking drugs, if that's what you're suggesting,' she told him angrily. 'I'm not *that* stupid, Ran.'

She closed her eyes momentarily, thinking painfully of David and the waste of his young life. No, drugs would never be something she would be tempted to use, and it hurt her that Ran thought she might.

The buoyancy and joy she had felt earlier had all gone, evaporated, burned away in the raw heat of Ran's anger and contempt. Suddenly she felt slightly tired and sick—the combination of no food, alcohol and too much painful emotion, she guessed miserably.

As tears filled her eyes she reached out impulsively, her fingers curling round the soft fabric of his shirt as she pleaded despairingly, 'Ran, *why* does it have to be like this between us? Why…can't we be friends…?'

'Friends…?'

She shrank back as she heard the bitterness in his voice.

'And what kind of friendship do you propose that we should have, Sylvie? The same kind you share with your *friend* who's just left? What's wrong? Isn't he satisfying you in bed? Do you need someone to compare him with? Because if so…'

Sylvie had had enough.

'That's not what I meant at all,' she cried out. 'I hate you, Ran… I hate you,' she told him tearfully, the child surfacing over the adult she had wanted to be…had wanted him to see…as she pummelled furiously at his chest, desperate to break down the barrier he had thrown up between them.

'Sylvie, stop it.'

As Ran caught hold of her small fists and held her away from him Sylvie realised what she was doing. Shamefaced, she started to look away from him, tensing in his hold when she heard him curse softly under his breath, and then suddenly he was sliding one hand into her hair, holding her head still as he bent his own towards hers, his breath fanning hotly against her face, her lips, his mouth...

His mouth!

In the shock of feeling Ran's mouth actually caressing her own, Sylvie immediately forgot everything which had preceded it— their quarrel, his anger and contempt—and remembered only her love for him!

Instinctively she moved closer to him, opening her mouth beneath his, responding joyously and passionately to his kiss, naively believing that despite everything that had happened he *must* care for her after all; he couldn't be kissing her like this and not do so, could he?

Innocently she pressed her body even closer to his, shivering in ecstatic pleasure as she felt her own response to his nearness. Beneath Alex's shirt, her breasts swelled and hardened; blissfully she anticipated Ran touching them, caressing them.

'*Ran.*'

His name was a soft plea whispered against his lips, her tongue-tip delicately touching them, exploring, tasting. She could feel him shuddering against her and, greatly daring, she darted her tongue into his mouth, seeking and then finding his, motivated, driven by instinct rather than knowledge; but the effect of her innocent exploration on Ran was so explosive that initially it took her off guard, half shocking and wholly exciting her. His hands started to move possessively over her body, down her back, shaping her waist and then moving lower to urge her lower body even closer to his as his tongue lunged repeatedly into the soft moistness of her mouth, carrying her inexorably to the point where she no longer had any control over either her emotions or her physical responsiveness to him, teaching her just what a world of difference existed between her own shyly tentative exploration of his mouth and his passionate male possession of hers.

Against her body she could feel the hard outline of his, and her whole body burned with virginal excitement as it registered and recognised the sensual heat of his physical arousal; the reality of what was happening between them rolled over her, engulfing and totally possessing her as she gave herself up willingly to its domination. She wanted to see him, touch him, taste him, *absorb* the reality of him with every single one of her senses. She wanted, needed, *craved*, to be fully a part of him; to have her whole body melt in the heat of their mutual passion so that she could be totally absorbed into him. She wanted...

With a small moan she wrenched herself away from him, her whole body trembling as she looked into his eyes and told him, *begged* him, 'Ran... Not here... I want... Take me to bed...' she whispered, her face flaming with the directness of her own request. But there was pride in her eyes, not shame, as she looked at him. Why *should* she feel ashamed of loving him so much? After all, he was the one who had kissed her...held her...

'Sylvie...'

The unexpected harshness in Ran's voice unnerved her a little, but she refused to pay any heed to it. Instead she walked up to him and, holding his eyes, very deliberately reached out and touched his body, intimately, there, just where she could see the way his arousal, his erection, was straining against his jeans.

She felt his reaction jolt right through him, as though her touch had burned him, but the drift of her fingertips had been as light as the wings of a butterfly.

'You want me, Ran,' she whispered shakily, 'and I want you…'

And then, without waiting for his response, she turned her back on him and walked very slowly and very deliberately to her bedroom door.

Once there she turned round and looked at him gravely.

He was still standing where she had left him, his face unfamiliarly pale, his eyes blazing with…

Quickly she looked away and then, before her courage could desert her, she tugged open the buttons of her borrowed shirt and shrugged it off.

Standing still and naked in full view of Ran whilst he watched her in silence was probably the hardest thing she had ever had to do, she acknowledged, but, somehow, doing it made her feel strong and brave and very, very womanly.

There was an odd glittering brilliance in Ran's eyes, and her stomach muscles tensed as she saw the way his jaw tightened as he looked away from her.

'Ran…' she commanded softly.

'Sylvie, for God's sake…'

Ignoring the tough grimness in his voice, she turned her back and walked fully into her small bedroom. Seconds later he had followed her there, slamming the bedroom door shut as he bent to retrieve her discarded shirt.

'Here. Put it back on,' he ordered curtly.

Sylvie looked at him.

He was standing just over an arm's length away from her and she could see that despite the hardness of his jaw his body was still aroused.

Uncertainly she licked her lips, tiny flames of excited

nervousness flicking along her spine as she saw the way his glance followed her involuntary movement.

'*You* put it on *for* me, Ran,' she whispered provocatively, taking a step towards him, and then another, and then, before she could stop herself, she discovered that *she* was the one looking at his mouth, and then at just where...

She heard him groan, saw out of the corner of her eye Alex's shirt as he hurled it away and then, blissfully, she was in his arms, her naked body pressed close against his fully dressed one as he covered her face, her throat, her mouth with hot, fevered kisses.

In his arms Sylvie shivered in mute delight. Every nerve-ending in her body was singing in joy and triumph.

'Oh Ran... Ran...' She whispered his name ecstatically as she wrapped her arms around him. 'I want you so much... I *love* you so much...' she told him, but she doubted he heard the words because they were silenced before she could properly form them as he continued to kiss her.

'I want you to take your clothes off,' she told him huskily when she finally could speak. 'I want to see all of you, Ran... I want...'

There was a hooded and unbelievably exciting look about his eyes as he stepped back from her and started to comply with her shy demand, never removing his glance from hers as he thrust off his clothes, his shirt first, revealing the hard-muscled expanse of his chest with its male pattern of silky dark hair. Sylvie caught her breath as she watched him. She had seen his bare torso before, had seen him in fact wearing little more than a pair of swimming shorts, but somehow this...this was different. Then his attitude towards his own semi-nudity had been laid-back and totally sexless; now...

Sylvie licked her lips a second time as she caught the burning look he was giving her.

His jeans followed his shirt and her stomach quivered, her heart leapt like a spawning salmon. Against the stark whiteness of his boxer shorts his skin gleamed, warmly tanned, and his body...his maleness...

Quickly she averted her eyes, suddenly conscious of her inexperience, her naiveté, her virginity, but her self-consciousness was quickly forgotten, swept away in a dizzying tide of longing and excitement. In another handful of seconds, less, she would be free to do what she had longed to do for what felt like for ever, free to look, to touch...to...

'Ran...'

Helplessly she closed the distance between them, rubbing her face blissfully against the soft warmth of his chest, breathing in the male scent of him in bemused adoration before shyly pressing her closed lips to his skin.

He felt so good, smelled so good; tentatively she opened her eyes and then her mouth, licking exploratively at his skin. In her ear she could feel the rapid increase in Ran's heartbeat. His arms tightened around her and then, suddenly, he was picking her up, carrying her over to the bed, laying her on it, touching her skin, stroking her body, kissing her in all the ways she had imagined and showing her at the same time just how far short of the wondrous reality her imagination had fallen.

In his hands her breasts swelled and ached, her nipples taut, begging to be touched, kissed, sucked.

Unable to stop herself, Sylvie started to moan softly

as his mouth tugged gently on her breast, her body arching, twisting, filled, *driven* by such an intensity of need that she herself was lost in it.

'Ran... Ran...'

Frantically she moaned his name against his hot skin, touching, licking, kissing as much of him as she could reach.

'Ran...*now*...please...*now*,' she heard herself demanding, even though part of her mind wondered just why she felt so overwhelmed by her own sense of urgency, by her own need to have the hot male strength of him buried deep inside her. She just knew that she did.

She could feel him touching her intimately with his fingers as he kissed her but she pushed them away. Everything that was female and intuitive within her urged her to reject something that was only a substitute for what her body, her nature, her essence, demanded, instinctively refusing a satisfaction which could not give her what nature had designed her for.

No completion, no conception could take place through what he was offering her and her body; her senses, her nature demanded what they believed was their due.

Without any previous experience to guide her Sylvie responded to her own instincts, lifting her hips, rubbing herself against him, moaning her urgent need until she felt Ran's hands move to her hips, holding her, lifting her as he finally moved against her.

A small tremor of shock made her gasp out loud, her body tensing and her eyes widening as she felt the reality of his body within hers. She had never really thought about the practicalities of sex...and he felt so...so male...so...so big...

She felt him check slightly and saw him frown, saw the recognition of her inexperience, her virginity, dawn in his eyes, but as he tried to draw back from her Sylvie wrapped herself around him, holding him, and then it was too late; then his body took over, demanding the satisfaction hers had been promising it.

It was everything and more that Sylvie had imagined—bliss, heaven...perfection, even if afterwards, as she curled up happily next to Ran, she did feel slightly sore... Slightly sore but oh, so deliciously pleased with herself. She was a *woman* now. Ran's woman... They would be married at Otel Place, of course, and Alex would give her away... Happily she drifted off to sleep.

In the morning when she woke up she was in bed alone, and at first she thought she must have dreamt the entire incident, but when she went padding into her living room she found Ran standing there fully dressed, staring out of the window. Overjoyed, she rushed over to him, flinging her arms around him, but instead of responding as she had expected, instead of turning round and holding her, kissing her, picking her up and carrying her back to bed, he firmly disengaged her arms and pushed her sternly away.

'What is it? What's wrong?' she demanded, not understanding. 'Last night—'

'Last night was a mistake,' Ran interrupted her curtly. 'It should never have happened and I wish to God... Why didn't you *tell* me you were still a virgin?'

'I... I...' Sylvie could feel her eyes starting to fill with tears.

This wasn't how it should be—Ran aloof, cold and distant, almost accusing.

'Ran, I love you,' she told him shakily. 'I want us to be together…married…'

'*Married?* You're a child still, Sylvie… Your mother…'

'I'm not a child, I'm nearly twenty,' she protested frantically.

'You're a *child*,' Ran insisted, 'and if I'd known… Why didn't you *tell* me? *Why* did you let me think that you and Wayne were lovers?'

'I *did* tell you but you wouldn't listen. I thought you'd be pleased…that you'd *want* to be the first…the only one…' she told him pathetically.

'*Pleased?* Oh, my God.' Ran started to laugh, a harshly bitter laugh. 'The only thing that could make this appalling situation any worse would be to discover that you're pregnant…'

Sylvie's face went white. Last night, lost in the throes of her love and their shared intimacy, she had craved the conception of his child, and to have to listen to him now, telling her that that was the last thing he wanted, that she was the last *person* he wanted, was the cruellest blow she had ever experienced.

'I'm on the pill,' she told him quietly, ducking her head as she explained, 'There were… I had… My doctor recommended it for other reasons.'

It was the truth, and it made her blood run cold now to remember how unwilling she had been to take it. Thank God she had. To have exposed a child, her child, to the dislike, the bitterness she could see in Ran's eyes and hear in his voice would have been more than she could bear.

All her dreams and her hopes lay in ruins around her, destroyed by Ran's rejection of her.

'Go and get dressed, please,' she heard him demanding. 'I have to leave soon, but first we need to talk.'

Get dressed!

Suddenly she felt as acutely self-conscious, as guilty as the first Eve must have done. As she tugged on her clothes in the privacy of her bedroom she knew that she had paid a heavy price for the intimacy of Ran's lovemaking—the loss not just of her innocence, but the destruction of her love, her faith, her belief in herself as a woman. She felt as though she never wanted to see Ran again, as though she could never bear to face him again, as though someone had wrenched away a protective curtain. She saw that last night could have been nothing more to him than the mere satisfying of a sexual itch, that *she* had been nothing more to him than someone, a *body*, to relieve his sexual frustration with.

As she walked back into the living room he handed her a mug of coffee. Taking it from him, she was careful to make sure that not only did her fingers not touch his but that they did not even touch the mug where his had done. She felt scorched, besmirched, *soiled* from the experience of knowing just how little he had actually wanted her. What she wanted more than anything else now was to get him out of here, out of her flat, out of her life, out of her heart for ever.

'Sylvie...'

'I don't want to talk about it, Ran,' she told him proudly, turning her back to him. 'It happened. It was a mistake, we both know that, but a girl has to lose her virginity some time...' She gave a small painful shrug.

'Wayne will be pleased. Like you, he didn't want to be the first…'

What on earth was she saying…implying…? Sylvie wondered sickly as her pride demanded, commanded, forced her to retaliate, lie and to convince Ran that he hadn't hurt her, that he couldn't possibly have the power to hurt her.

'You begged *me* to make love to you so that you could have sex with Wayne?'

She could hear disbelief and something else in the harsh fury of Ran's voice, but shakily she ignored it, holding up her head as she turned round to confront him.

'Yes, that's right,' she agreed.

'I don't believe you,' Ran told her flatly, adding grimly, 'You said you loved me. You were even talking about marriage…'

Sylvie gave a small dismissive shrug.

'Isn't that what a *virgin* is supposed to do?' She pulled an uncaring face. 'How could I possibly love *you*, Ran? Why *should* I love you? All you ever do is criticise me. I want you to leave…'

'Sylvie, you can't just—'

'Wayne will be coming round soon,' she fibbed, adding carelessly, 'He's been telling me for ages to find someone to…to lose my virginity with. He's very experienced and he likes his lovers to know…to know what sex is all about…Wayne's the man I love.'

What was she *saying*? Sylvie could hardly believe the lies she was hearing herself speak, but Ran seemed to have no difficulty in accepting them.

Slamming down his barely touched mug of coffee, he came towards her.

Immediately Sylvie backed away.

'I don't know why you're making such a fuss,' she told him, adding flippantly, 'It's no big deal after all—'

'No…maybe not to you,' Ran interrupted her grimly.

'Not to you either,' Sylvie told him. Her phone started to ring and she hurried towards it, telling him over her shoulder, 'That will be Wayne…'

It wasn't, and she knew that the poor double-glazing salesperson must have been astonished and probably shocked by the tone of her conversation as she overrode his sales pitch, telling him that she had done what he wanted and that she couldn't wait to see him, to be with him properly, if he knew what she meant. Blowing noisy kisses into the receiver, she ended the call and then turned to Ran, telling him coolly, 'Wayne's on his way, so unless you want to stand and watch to see just how quick a learner I am…'

She was still smiling—the hurting, false, ridiculous smile she had pinned to her face as she'd challenged him—when she heard the door slam behind him, and then continued to wear it for several minutes after he had gone, despite the fact that tears were flooding from her eyes.

It was later that morning that she actually bumped into Wayne, completely by chance. In the two hours since Ran had left she had had more than enough time to dwell on what had happened and what she had said, and by the time she saw Wayne she had convinced herself that it was totally impossible for her ever to see Ran again…ever to see *anyone* again who was even remotely connected with him.

'Hi there, doll,' Wayne greeted her with a grin. 'Looks like it's time to say goodbye. I'm meeting up with the eco-warriors this afternoon.'

Swiftly Sylvie made up her mind, seizing on the opportunity to make her escape, not just from Ran but from everything that was associated with him—her love, her shame, and her fear that he would somehow guess that she had lied to him.

'I'm coming with you,' she told Wayne determinedly, adding before he could argue, 'My stepbrother has sent me some money so I can afford to support myself.'

'How much has he sent you?' Wayne questioned her interestedly.

An hour later, having packed everything that she would need, Sylvie locked the door of her flat behind her and went to join Wayne, who was waiting in his car.

She was a new Sylvie now, a different Sylvie. Ran, her love for him, the life she had once led—*all* were in the past and best forgotten.

CHAPTER SEVEN

A NOISE in the garden outside her window brought Sylvie out of her reverie. Startled, she let her unfocused gaze sweep the moonlit darkness and then sweep it again, her body stiffening as she saw Ran turn away and disappear into the shadows.

How long had he been standing there watching her? She knew from his clothes that he must have been working, probably checking for poachers who, she guessed, were as much a potential threat here as they had often been on her stepbrother's estate.

Shivering, she headed back to her bed. It was gone three o'clock in the morning and as she touched her face she realised that it was wet with her tears.

Why in heaven's name did she have to be so pathetic…standing there with tears pouring down her face whilst she relived the pain of the past? Oh, but she envied Ran. Her mouth twisted into a bitter smile as she tried to imagine *him* ever crying a single tear over her.

What had happened to her will-power, her strength; to the promise she had made herself before coming here—that things were going to be different, that never again would Ran be allowed to treat her with the same contempt he had shown her when they had faced one another as foes, enemies, on opposite sides, when she had allowed the eco-warriors to invade Alex's land, to destroy the pretty woodland glade that she had once worked so hard to help create…just as Ran had destroyed her love and also destroyed her?

He had hated her for that almost as much as she had hated him. She had seen it in his eyes when he'd insisted on joining the others to see her off to America.

'Why are you here?' she had taunted.

'Why do you think?' he had responded, and of course she had known. He wanted to be sure that she really was leaving.

And now she was back—back to make the unwanted and agonisingly painful discovery that some things *didn't* change, that some loves didn't die.

She wasn't twenty any longer; it was impossible for her to run away now, to take refuge in disappearing, as she'd tried to escape herself and her love. She had a job to do, responsibilities, and besides, what had running away the first time actually achieved? It hadn't stopped her loving him, had it?

In the protective darkness of the moonlit garden Ran leaned back against the trunk of a concealing tree and closed his eyes. The discovery that Sylvie was going to be representing the Trust had reinforced all the irony he had felt when he had first learnt of his unexpected inheritance. He might not be a millionaire, but his lifestyle now and his prospects were certainly a far cry from what they had been when Sylvie's mother had insisted on Alex speaking to him about Sylvie's youthful crush on him.

He had been aware, of course, of her feelings, aware of them and aware too that at seventeen she was far too young, far too emotionally immature for the sort of relationship that he, as a man in his twenties, might have wanted.

'What the hell does Sylvie's mother think I'm going to *do*?' he had demanded angrily as he'd paced the floor of Alex's library.

Sympathetically Alex had shaken his head as he'd told him quietly, 'This isn't exactly easy for me, Ran. You're my friend as well as—'

'Your *employee*...' Angrily Ran had grimaced. 'No doubt as far as Sylvie's mother is concerned I'm only one step removed from being a servant,' he had expostulated scornfully.

Wisely, Alex had said nothing, allowing him to express his ire and distaste instead.

'You must share her concern,' he had concluded, 'otherwise you wouldn't have raised the subject.'

'Yes, in some ways I do,' Alex had agreed steadily. 'Not, I hardly need say, because I think you are in any way socially inferior to Sylvie. I know your family background, Ran, and your lineage, and if there's any shortfall of social acceptability here it's far more on Sylvie's side than yours. But I hope you know me well enough to know that that kind of attitude is totally abhorrent to me. No, my concern lies in a rather different direction and, in all honesty, it's Sylvie I should more properly be speaking to and not you, but...well, she isn't my sister, there's no blood tie between us, and teenage girls and their emotions are, I'm afraid, somewhat outside my own limited experience. So...the truth is that Sylvie believes herself in love with you with all the ferocity that teenagers do believe in such things. For your sake as much as for hers I feel that such feelings are best not...encouraged. She's young and very vulnerable and I should hate to see her hurt...to see either of you hurt,' he had amended gently when he had seen Ran's expression.

'What the hell do you think I'm going to do to her?' Ran had exploded. 'Take her to bed and...?'

'Is it really so impossible that you might be tempted to?' Alex had asked him quietly. 'I'm not criticising or condemning, Ran; physically she's mature and she loves you—or believes she does—'

'She's got a crush on me that she'll soon grow out of,' Ran had interrupted him grimly. 'That's what you want me to say, isn't it? And I should keep my hands off her until she does grow out of it...out of me... But what if *I* feel differently, Alex? What if *I* want...?' He had shaken his head, angry with himself as well as with Alex. *More* angry with himself than he was with Alex who he knew was only doing what he saw as his duty by his stepsister.

'You're right, she's a child still, and the sooner she grows up and forgets all about me the better,' Ran had told him hardily. 'And as for taking her to bed,' he had thrown at Alex as he turned to leave, 'well, there's always a cure for that.'

And so there had been, for a while at least, until he had grown sickened and shamed by the emptiness of the sexual encounters he was sharing with women who meant as little to him emotionally as he did to them. And, even with that form of release, keeping the promise he had made to Alex and himself hadn't been easy. There had been times, far too many of them, when he had nearly weakened, like when he had fished her out of the muddy lake and taken her back to his cottage. Oh, God, the temptation then to take what she was so innocently offering him, to take on the role not so much of seducer as sorcerer, transmuting the frail strength of her youthful crush on him into the enduring bond of real adult love.

But, despite the temptation which kissing her had presented, somehow he had always managed to tell himself of the differences that lay between them in age, experience and in prospects. He loved his job and wouldn't have wanted to change it for anything or *anyone*, but there was no denying that to expect a girl, brought up as Sylvie had been with every conceivable luxury, to move into the kind of accommodation estate managers normally occupied, to live the often lonely lifestyle that would be hers when he was working… He just couldn't do it. Had she been older, wiser…poorer…it might have been different. And so he had resisted the temptation to give in to her desire and his own love, and he had praised himself for his selflessness, until the fateful day he had taken her Alex's cheque.

To see her there, outside her flat, dressed only in a man's shirt—a shirt through which, with the hot summer sunshine slanting down on her, he could see quite plainly the shape and fullness of her breasts and even the dark aureoles of her nipples—to watch her with another man, a man who he had immediately assumed was her lover, had created within him an anger, a bitterness, a jealousy that had rent wide apart his self-control.

To discover later, *too* late, that there had been no other lover, to realise what he had done and why, had filled him with such self-loathing that he could hardly endure the weight of his own guilt.

'I love you,' Sylvie had told him innocently. 'I want us to be together…'

He had spent the previous week with Alex, discussing

ways and means in which they could reduce the cost of running the estate. Amongst them had been his own suggestion that they rent out his cottage and that he move into rooms in the main house. He knew that if Alex accepted his suggestion he wouldn't even have a proper home to offer her. He could just imagine how her mother would react to that, to the idea of her daughter living in rooms above the stables of the house where she had been brought up. And Sylvie was still so young, still so naive...still at university with the whole of her life in front of her. What right had *he* to use what had happened between them to tie her to him? No, better to let her think that he didn't want her than to have her turn to him five or even ten years down the line to tell him that she had made a mistake; to accuse him of putting his own emotions before her needs, of taking advantage of her youth and inexperience.

And he'd been glad he had done so when she had dropped the bombshell about her relationship with Wayne.

Somehow that was something he had just not expected, but he had seen from the expression in her eyes and the vehemence in her voice that she meant every word she was saying. And so he had walked away, telling himself that it was for the best for her, best that somehow, some time, some *way* he should learn how to forget her.

But, of course, he had never done so.

And now here she was, back in his life, a woman now and not a girl, and what a woman, how much of a woman, *the* woman whom he loved—and who hated him.

It had hurt him more than he could bear that she

should think he would actually try to cheat anyone...
Did her precious Lloyd know how lucky he was or how
much he, Ran, would give simply to hold her in his arms
and hear her telling him that she loved him? He would
give everything he had, everything he was...

What a fool he was. She didn't love him, she *loathed*
him.

Watching her just now on his way back from checking
on the fences, on the look-out for potential poachers, he
had ached so badly for her, so very, *very* badly. There
was no point in him going to bed; soon the false dawn
would be lightening the night sky, and besides, there was
only one reason he wanted to be in bed right now and
it had nothing to do with sleeping or being alone.

Kissing her tonight had opened the floodgates on his
love for her and his body still ached with the longing it
had evoked. How the hell he was going to get through
the next few months he had no idea. Grimly he turned
away from the house and the temptation of Sylvie's bedroom, Sylvie's bed, Sylvie herself.

CHAPTER EIGHT

'HI, HON, it's me, Lloyd.'

Sylvie smiled warmly as she recognised her boss's voice.

'Lloyd,' she responded, 'how are you?'

'Fine, I guess. Listen, I've got to come over to England on some other business and I thought whilst I was there I'd drive up to Derbyshire and see how you're getting on with Haverton Hall.'

Sylvie laughed. She wasn't in the least deceived. Lloyd was like a child with a new toy whenever he acquired a new property, saying every time that he wasn't going to visit it again until all the renovation work had been complete and then being totally unable to resist checking on how things were going. Or not so much checking on how things were going, but sneaking another look, like a child sneaking a look at a hidden-away Christmas present just to check that it was still there and that he was actually going to receive it. As Sylvie well knew, no matter how many properties Lloyd acquired, he still continued to fall in love with new ones, and Haverton Hall was well worth falling in love with.

This morning she had an appointment with the firm who were going to work on the restoration of the carving and the plasterwork. Based in London, the artisans the firm employed had all completed their training at the same Italian firm that Sylvie had used when renovating the *palazzo*. She had seen samples and photographs of

126

their work and knew that no matter how expensive they might be—and they would be—they were the right people to work on Haverton Hall.

'When are you arriving?' she asked Lloyd, still smiling.

'I'm booked on today's Concorde,' he told her.

Sylvie heard the door to the small office she had organised for herself at Haverton Hall open behind her, but she didn't turn round. She didn't need to; she knew from the reaction of her own body that it was Ran who had walked in. Ever since the night he had kissed her and they had argued, they had treated one another with cold distance. She had gone downstairs that morning to discover a neat file of papers and bank statements awaiting her which proved conclusively that Ran had paid for the work done on the Rectory himself.

She had apologised, very formally and very curtly, and then pointed out that he wouldn't have been the first client to take advantage of Lloyd's generosity.

'*I* haven't taken advantage of it,' he'd reminded her acidly, before walking away from her.

Since then, the contact between them had been as minimal as both of them could make it.

'Oh, Lloyd, that's wonderful,' she told her employer truthfully. 'I've missed you.' It was true. She had missed him and suddenly something occurred to her. 'Look, I've got to come down to London to see some people. Why don't we drive back together? I'm going to have to stay overnight anyway... The Annabelle?' she responded, when he told her where he was planning to stay, and then teased him, 'Isn't that a bit romantic...?'

'I've heard some good things about its designer,'

Lloyd responded mock-sternly. 'My interest in the place is purely professional.'

By the time Sylvie had completed her telephone call Ran had gone. Good; the less contact she had with him the better. She much preferred her solitary evening meals to the trauma of spending any time with him, even if she did sometimes wonder *where* he was eating and with whom and if he stayed with her all night. It had to be Vicky, of course. The woman was forever telephoning him, purring smugly down the line whenever Sylvie answered, demanding, 'Tell Ran to ring me; he's got my number.'

She was sure he had, Sylvie had decided acidly, him and every other man who was subjected to the divorcee's high octane blend of sexuality.

The shop occupied by Messrs Phillips and Company, master gilders and restorers, was down a narrow alley, a small courtyard of buildings that time seemed to have forgotten.

Walking into the courtyard was like walking back in time, Sylvie decided as she gasped in delight at the Elizabethan framework of the narrow buildings with their outward-jutting upper storeys.

'They belong to one of the royal estates,' the chief partner in the business, Stuart Phillips, informed Sylvie. 'And they're very strict, not just about the maintenance of the building but about who they take as tenants as well. We got our tenancy after we had been commissioned to work on one of the royal palaces.'

An hour later, after Sylvie had discussed Haverton Hall and the work required on it, he turned to her and told her, 'We *can* do it, but it's going to be very costly.'

'Very costly is fine,' Sylvie assured him and then smiled at him as she added softly, '*Exorbitantly* costly isn't; there's enough work here to keep you in business for nearly twelve months...guaranteed work.'

'Our order books are already full,' he told her urbanely.

'Not according to my contacts,' Sylvie retaliated. 'The way I heard it, one of your biggest contracts has been withdrawn due to lack of funds.'

'I don't know who your informants are...' Stuart Phillips began huffily, but Sylvie stopped him.

'Let's be honest with one another, shall we?' she suggested firmly. 'We're both busy people with no time to waste on silly point-scoring. You're the best in the business in this country and I *want* the best for Haverton Hall, but...there are other firms...'

'We shall need a guarantee that the contract will be seen through to its end,' he told her, frowning. 'I don't like carrying all my eggs in one basket...'

'You shall have it,' Sylvie assured him.

'Mmm... From the records you've shown us the original workmanship was done to a very high standard, especially the wood-carving.'

'If not Grinling Gibbons himself, then certainly one of his most skilful pupils,' Sylvie agreed.

'The records you've got of the original designed decor are excellent; they even list the furniture and each room's colour scheme,' he assessed.

She had Ran to thank for that, Sylvie acknowledged. Normally it fell to her lot to search painstakingly through the records to put together a composite picture of what a property had originally looked like. On this occasion Ran had done all that spadework for her. Not that she had allowed him to see how impressed she was. She wasn't prepared to do *anything* that would allow him to think he had some sort of advantage over her.

When the time came for her and Stuart Phillips to part company Sylvie had his agreement to concentrate exclusively on the work on Haverton Hall, even though she had had to agree to a substantial bonus payment to get him to do so. She made sure she held tightly to budget where she could, but she would never take the less expensive option when it came to employing the best craftsmen. It would be worth it, she exulted as she left the courtyard. Haverton Hall was worth it.

She had arranged to meet Lloyd at his hotel for afternoon tea. He loved that type of tradition and, as he happily informed her an hour later when she was shown up to his private suite, 'No other country serves an afternoon tea quite like England…'

'I should hope not,' was Sylvie's tongue-in-cheek response, then she started to tell him about her visit to the gilders.

'You're sure they'll be as good as the Italians?' he asked her at one point, suddenly very professional and alert.

'Better,' Sylvie told him simply. 'You see, the original work on the house was carried out by *English* workmen who had trained in Italy, rather like Messrs Phillips, artisans, and my guess is that their workmanship, although Italian in conception, would have had a decidedly English interpretation to it—where an Italian craftsman might have carved cherubs and allegorical scenes from the great masters, an English craftsman would have carved animals and birds, things from *nature*.'

'Why don't you stay here tonight?' Lloyd suggested

once they had finished talking about her visit to Messrs Phillips and Company. 'I can ring down and book you a room.'

Sylvie shook her head.

'No, thanks; I've already arranged to stay overnight with my mother.'

Knowing that Lloyd had a business dinner organized, Sylvie left just after five o'clock, having arranged to pick him up at ten in the morning.

She drove to her mother's, suffering the latter's perfumed embrace after her mother's maid had let her into the apartment.

'Darling, it's my bridge evening this evening. I could cancel it but...'

'No, please don't.' Sylvie checked her mother with a smile.

'Well, at least we can have dinner together and you can tell me all your news. How is dear Ran? So exciting, his inheritance...the title...'

Sylvie's smile faded.

'Ran's fine,' she told her mother, adding dismissively, 'We don't see an awful lot of one another; we're both busy.'

'Oh, darling, such a shame,' her mother protested.

'I...' Sylvie gave her a direct look. 'At one time you thoroughly disapproved of him.' And my feelings for him, Sylvie could have added, but she didn't.

Her mother made a small *moue*. 'But, darling, that was before...'

'Before what?' Sylvie challenged her wryly. 'Before he inherited the title...'

'Well, these things *do* make a difference.' Her mother

defended herself as Sylvie gave her a quizzical look. 'Ran is now an extremely eligible man.'

'Mother! These days a woman doesn't need an eligible man,' Sylvie told her. 'We can support ourselves.'

'Every woman needs a man to love her, Sylvie,' her mother told her sadly. 'I still miss your stepfather.'

Immediately Sylvie was contrite. Her mother was old-fashioned and out of touch in her ideas, her thinking, but she had genuinely loved both Sylvie's own father and her second husband, Alex's father, and Sylvie knew that despite the business with which she filled her days she was sometimes lonely.

'Have you seen Alex and Mollie recently?' she questioned, wanting to turn the conversation into happier channels.

'Oh, yes,' her mother responded immediately and warmly, 'and they've invited me to Otel Place for Christmas.'

Several hours later, as she prepared for an early night, Sylvie wondered what Ran was doing. Not going to bed on his own if his recent behaviour pattern was to be followed. Angrily, she closed her eyes. What did it matter to her who Ran spent his nights with or how?

What did it matter?

All the world, *that* was how much it mattered, but no one but her must ever know that.

Even before he had kissed her she had known the truth. Just the way her body, her senses, her being, had reacted the moment she had set eyes on him again had told her that what she had tried to dismiss as a mere childish crush had somewhere, somehow, against all the odds and certainly against her own will, turned into real adult love. She ached for Ran—to be at one with him, at peace with him, to be *loved* by him, to share his life, to bear his children—with such an intensity that sometimes she didn't know quite how she was going to be able to go on bearing it.

Live one day at a time, that was her present motto; just get through each minute, each hour, just go on telling herself that ultimately it was going to get better, that once the work on Haverton Hall was finished and she was out of Ran's orbit she would be able to rebuild her defences and, with them, her own life. That was what she told herself, but deep down inside she wasn't sure she truly believed it.

'We'll have to call at the Rectory first,' Sylvie warned Lloyd as she drove north. 'I don't have the keys to Haverton Hall with me.'

'That's fine by me,' Lloyd assured her. 'How are you and Ran getting along, by the way?'

'He's a client of the Trust,' Sylvie pointed out severely.

'So you haven't fallen in love with him, then,' Lloyd teased her. Somehow Sylvie managed to force a responsive smile. Lloyd meant no harm. He took a paternal interest in her and often told her, only semi-jokingly, that it was time she fell in love. He had no idea about the real state of affairs between her and Ran, the real state of her heart, her emotions.

'Say, this is really beautiful countryside,' he commented as they drove through Derbyshire.

'But still not as beautiful as Haverton,' Sylvie teased him.

Immediately he was off, enthusing about the house and its architecture.

Sylvie's heart sank when she pulled up outside the Rectory and saw that Ran's Land Rover was there. There was another car outside as well and Sylvie's heart dropped even further when she recognised it. Perhaps with her away and the opportunity to have the house to themselves, Ran and Vicky had decided on a change of venue and had spent the night together here.

Ran had given her a set of keys to the Rectory, and rather than disturb him she used them to unlock the door, but to her discomfort, as they walked through the hall, Ran and Vicky were just coming downstairs.

'Hi there,' Lloyd began genially, but before Ran could say anything his telephone began to ring.

'Excuse me a moment, will you?' he said apologetically, leaving the three of them together as he hurried into the library to answer the telephone.

'I don't think we've met,' Vicky began coyly, ignoring Sylvie to smile provocatively at Lloyd.

'Lloyd, Vicky Edwards.' Sylvie introduced them mechanically. 'Lloyd is my boss and—'

'So you work for the Trust as well, do you?' Vicky commented.

'Lloyd *is* the Trust,' Sylvie told her, thoroughly exasperated by the other woman's manner.

'Oh…how very interesting,' she responded softly, immediately crossing the hall to Lloyd's side, turning her back on Sylvie. 'You must tell me more…'

Quite how Vicky managed to invite herself to join them when they went to Haverton Sylvie wasn't quite sure, but invite herself she most certainly had.

Lloyd obviously didn't share her own dislike of her, she recognised as she saw the bemused male appreciation with which he was regarding the older woman.

By the time Ran rejoined them Vicky was purring seductively to Lloyd.

'So you're staying at the Annabelle. I've heard it's the last word in luxury…'

'It sure is,' Lloyd agreed enthusiastically. 'My suite is really something else, isn't it, Sylvie?'

'Yes, it is,' Sylvie agreed colourlessly. Out of the corner of her eye she could see Ran switching his concentration from Lloyd and Vicky to her, frowning as he did so.

It wasn't *her* fault that his lady-friend, his *lover*, was showing an interest in Lloyd… Sylvie had seen women expressing such an interest before, of course; Lloyd was an extremely wealthy man and a very, very charming one. In the past he had often made a joke of their pursuit of him, warning Sylvie that it was part of her job to keep them at bay. For his age he was extremely fit and physically he looked attractive. He still had a full head of silver hair and his eyes held a warm twinkle, but to prefer him to Ran… Or was it perhaps his bank balance that was attracting the other woman? Sylvie wondered unkindly.

In the end, all four of them drove over to Haverton Hall in Ran's Land Rover, with Vicky pulling a small face as she coaxed Lloyd to sit in the back with her.

'This really is the most uncomfortable old thing, Ran,' she complained, adding to Lloyd in a sugary sweet voice, 'I keep telling him he should buy himself a decent four-wheel drive. In all the years I've known Ran, he's never owned a decent car. You Americans make such wonderful ones…so luxurious and comfortable…'

'Well, I guess we have the country for them,' Lloyd agreed with a smile. 'You and Ran are old friends then?'

Vicky pouted.

'Well, we certainly go back a long way—although I only moved to Derbyshire a short time ago and, by co-incidence, I discovered that Ran was one of my new neighbours and we were able to renew old acquain-tances.'

Some coincidence, Sylvie reflected ironically, irritated by Vicky's behaviour. What on earth did Ran see in her? Surely he could see what type of woman she was—how unworthy of him she was?

When they arrived at Haverton Hall, Vicky made a big performance of climbing out of the Land Rover, thanking Lloyd effusively for helping her, leaning heavily on his arm as she complained about the uneven gravel on the forecourt.

'You should have worn flat shoes like Sylvie,' Ran told her.

'Flat shoes…? Ugh, no, never.' She shuddered. 'I *always* wear high heels,' she confided to Lloyd. 'I think they're so much more feminine.' Lifting her foot, she held out one slim, elegant ankle for his inspection.

'Very pretty,' Lloyd approved, 'but you'd better hang onto me. We don't want you to hurt yourself.'

As they toured the house, Sylvie's irritation with Vicky grew. Every time she made a comment, Vicky had to chip in, diverting Lloyd's attention from the house to herself, accompanying each successful attempt to do so with a look of acid triumph in Sylvie's direction. Really, the woman was totally impossible. They weren't in competition for his approval...his *affections*, for goodness' sake. She was simply trying to do her job. If Ran's lover wanted to flirt with Lloyd, that was totally her business and Ran's. All that Sylvie wished was that she had chosen another time to do so.

'The Annabelle sounds the most fabulous hotel. I'd love to see it... I've been planning to go to London for some time... I need some new clothes and there's nowhere in Derbyshire.' Vicky gave a small, fastidious shudder as they finally headed back to the Land Rover.

'You were? Say, why don't you come back with me, then? Sylvie's going to drive me to Manchester airport and—' Lloyd began politely.

'Come to London and stay at the Annabelle as your guest...?' Vicky pounced immediately. 'Oh, how wonderful and how kind of you. I'd love to...' she breathed huskily.

Sylvie, who guessed that Lloyd had simply been suggesting that they travel together, could only marvel at the other woman's sang-froid and her cheek. *She* would never have dared to behave as Vicky had just done. But Lloyd, far from looking displeased, was almost beaming from ear to ear.

Sylvie waited until they were back at the Rectory and Vicky had disappeared to 'tidy herself up' before taking Lloyd to one side, out of Ran's earshot, to warn him discreetly, 'Lloyd, Vicky is Ran's girlfriend and I don't think—'

'So far as I am concerned, Vicky is a free agent. If she wants to go to London with Lloyd then that's up to her.' Sylvie bit her lip as Ran interrupted her. He had been on the other side of the hallway, but then his hearing had always been extremely sharp. It went with his job.

'I'm afraid I'm going to have to go home and collect a few things,' Vicky apologised gushingly to Lloyd as she came back downstairs. 'I don't want to keep you waiting.'

Grimly Sylvie watched as she batted heavily mascaraed eyelashes in Lloyd's direction.

'No problem,' he assured her. 'There are a few things Sylvie and I need to discuss and I guess Ran too. You take all the time you need, my dear.'

'I expect the Annabelle is very dressy,' Vicky murmured appreciatively.

'Charming woman,' Lloyd commented warmly after she had gone.

'Yes, she is,' Ran agreed.

'About as charming as a piranha,' Sylvie muttered between clenched teeth behind their backs before reminding Lloyd curtly, 'I've got preliminary estimates for some of the work here if you want to see them. I have faxed copies off to New York, but...'

'Sylvie, you're so efficient,' Lloyd told her, smiling benignly at her. 'I keep telling her, Ran, that she needs to relax a bit more...have fun... When was the last time *you* spent a day shopping for yourself?' he challenged her before she could say anything.

'I shopped in Italy,' she told him dismissively.

'Yes, I know. I was there, remember...? I took her to Armani,' he told Ran. 'And what did she do? She told me that the clothes were far too expensive. What do you do with a woman like that?'

'They *were* too expensive,' Sylvie told him defensively. Too expensive for her at any rate, and although she knew that Lloyd would happily have offered to buy an outfit for her he was still her employer and she had no intention of taking advantage of his generosity. Even so, it hurt to know that he was comparing her to Vicky Edwards and perhaps finding her less feminine, less womanly, and in front of *Ran*. It was plain what both of them were thinking: that somehow she was less *fun* than the other woman—less of a *woman*. Well, let them think what they liked, she decided angrily. *She* was there to do a job, not to…to flirt and bat her eyelashes.

'She's a wonderful girl,' she heard Lloyd telling Ran as she went to get the papers she wanted him to see. 'But she works too hard, takes life too seriously.'

After she had dropped Lloyd and Vicky off at the airport, her head aching from listening to the other woman's flirtatious comments, instead of heading back to Derbyshire, Sylvie drove on impulse to Manchester itself and parked the Discovery outside the Emporio Armani boutique that a kindly taxi driver had directed her to.

A pretty, dark-haired girl who could have been Italian but wasn't brought her the trouser suit she had seen in the window.

The diffusion range might be cheaper than the designer originals but it was still expensive. Even so… As she turned and twisted in front of the mirror, studying her reflection in the flatteringly cut suit, Sylvie admitted that she couldn't resist it. Neither could she resist the matching shirt that went with it.

So, she was dull and boring and unfeminine, was she? Well, she might not wear three-inch heels, and she certainly didn't flutter her eyelashes, but she was still a woman…very much a woman…more than woman enough to ache with longing for Ran. Oh, yes, she was more than woman enough for that!

CHAPTER NINE

'YOU'VE been a long time. What happened?'

Guiltily Sylvie spun round, dropping her Armani carrier bag as she did so. She had arrived back at the Rectory five minutes ago and had decided to go straight to her room, but she had just reached the top of the stairs when Ran emerged from his room, his curt comment coupled with her own guilt startling her.

'You've been shopping,' he said sharply in disbelief, answering his own question as he saw the bag she had just dropped and the contents spilled out from it onto the carpet.

'What if I have?' Sylvie retorted defensively, bending down to gather up her purchases but not fast enough to match Ran, who had bent and got there before her, scooping up the soft, expensive cloth and then, pausing, shocking her by removing it completely from the carrier. He studied what she had bought and then lifted his gaze to her flushed face.

'New clothes. Now, then, I wonder what motivated you to do that?' he asked her softly.

'What I choose to do with my time and my money is no business of yours,' Sylvie snapped sharply at him.

But he ignored her, taunting her softly, 'What exactly are you trying to do, Sylvie? Compete with Vicky? You can't. You don't have the right type of...assets.'

Furious with him, and with herself because his taunting remarks weren't just making her angry, they were hurting her badly as well, Sylvie exploded into angry self-defence.

'If by "the right type of assets" you mean I don't use my womanhood, my sexuality, as some kind of...of cheap means of attracting men, then I'm glad to say that I don't,' she agreed.

'Really? Then why go and buy this?' Ran challenged her softly, indicating the trouser suit.

'I bought it on impulse,' she told him quickly. Too quickly, she realised as she saw the cynical look he was giving her. 'Anyway,' she added protectively, 'it's hardly the kind of outfit a woman would buy to...to attract a man...'

'No?' Ran gave her a sardonic smile. 'Oh, come on, Sylvie, we both know better than that. There's something powerfully alluring about the sight of a woman wearing a trouser suit, something very, very sensual and appealing—much more so than an over-tight dress on an over-exposed body. You bought this outfit because you're jealous of Vicky. Because you—'

'Me...jealous...of her?' Sylvie virtually spat at him as she grabbed her new purchase from him and stuffed it back into the bag. 'No way,' she told him, shaking her head almost violently in denial. 'Why should I be jealous?' she added dangerously, too upset to question the wisdom of inviting him to humiliate her still further by revealing his awareness of just how she felt about him. 'Just because years ago I was stupid enough, adoring enough, *vulnerable* enough to...to care too much about you, that doesn't mean that I'm jealous of your lover. In fact...'

'My *lover*?' Ran stopped her as they both stood up, frowning down at her as he informed her curtly, 'I was referring to the fact that you're jealous because you're afraid of losing *Lloyd* to Vicky. He's your lover and—'

'My lover...? Lloyd?' Sylvie stared at him in disbelief.

Suddenly Sylvie had had enough. There was no way that Ran could possibly, genuinely, believe that she and Lloyd were lovers; he was just playing some kind of peculiar and cruel game with her. Well, he was going to have to play it on his own. Grabbing hold of her shopping, she darted past him, almost running into her bedroom and slamming the door behind her, her heart thudding with angry pain.

As she closed her eyes and leaned against the door she had just closed, she could feel them starting to burn with the useless demeaning tears of her unwanted love.

What was Ran doing now—laughing inwardly at her because he knew that her jealousy, her pain, her *love* were all for him, or was he too wrapped up in what he thought to spare any time to consider her feelings? Had he accused her of being jealous out of his own feelings of jealousy against Lloyd?

This job, which she had taken on with such high hopes, such a surge of determination and conviction that through it she would finally and for ever slay the dragons of her tormented youthful love for him, had now turned into a hydra-headed monster which she could never hope to overcome. How on earth was she going to be able to concentrate on what she had to do when she was forced to work in such close proximity to Ran?

No. It was impossible, she acknowledged half an hour later as she sat at her desk trying to concentrate on the work schedule she had in front of her. No matter how hard she tried to visualise a situation where she and Ran could work together in harmony, her emotions untouched by his presence, all she could actually see was a situation that was going to get worse and worse as she became more and more helplessly trapped in her love and his lack of it. The best remedy, the only remedy she could honestly see that would work would be for her to go to Lloyd and ask him to find someone else to complete this project, she admitted unhappily.

It wasn't a course she wanted to take. She prided herself on her professionalism and it would mean taking Lloyd into her confidence about her feelings for Ran— she knew, of course, that he would respect them, but even so...

If she stayed on the possibility was—no, the *probability* was, she corrected herself fiercely, that sooner or later she would make a mistake that could prejudice the progress of the work on the house. This was a project that was going to demand her total concentration and attention and how could she give it when all the time she was thinking about Ran, when her feelings for him were already dominating her mind and her emotions?

It wasn't going to be easy. She hated letting Lloyd down; in fact, it felt as though in asking him to find someone else to take over this particular project for her she was letting *herself* down; but she feared that if she stayed the way in which she could potentially let herself down, damage herself and her self-esteem, her very *self*, could be far more traumatic.

The anger and contempt which Ran had displayed towards her this evening had shown how very little compassion he was likely to have for her. No, there was no other way.

It was with a very heavy heart that Sylvie prepared

for bed. There would be other houses, other projects, and no one but her would ever know how much it would hurt knowing that it was someone else who would have the pleasure of restoring Ran's ancestral home to what it must once have been, just as it would be another woman who would ultimately stand beside Ran and their children in love and pride as they went through their lives together.

Ran wasn't sure just what had woken him up first—his training, his work, meant that he was always alert to any sound that heralded some unfamiliarity, his perceptions and senses so keenly attuned that he was aware of such changes even in his sleep.

Alert and wide awake, he lay in the darkness listening. The illuminated face of his alarm clock showed that it was just gone half past one in the morning. The house had no alarm system. Lucy, his gun dog who slept downstairs, might be getting on in years now but she would have been barking if someone had been trying to break into the house, and besides, the outside lights had not come on.

Through his open bedroom window he could hear an owl hooting as it flew past. No alien sounds disturbed the natural busyness of the country night.

He started to relax and then he heard it—a door opening upstairs. Immediately he was out of bed and, reaching for his robe, pulled it on—he slept nude—before striding across to open his bedroom door quietly.

He saw her immediately, a slim white wraith who seemed to float rather than walk down the corridor, but, ethereal though she looked, Sylvie was no ghost. Even before he reached her he knew that she was sleepwalking; all the tell-tale signs were there, and of course he knew from her girlhood exactly what to do. So why was it so hard, then, to take her gently in his hold so that he could turn her round and walk her back to her bedroom?

The best thing to do, they had all been told after the first frightening occasion when she had been found wandering the long gallery at Otel Place, totally oblivious to what she was doing, was to guide her gently back to bed, if possible without waking her; but now, as he touched her, Ran could feel her start to tremble violently, her face turning towards him, her body stiffening as he tried to turn her round. Cursing under his breath, he glanced towards his own still open bedroom door. Perhaps if he could get her in there… The old family doctor at Otel Place had recommended that she be allowed to wake up naturally rather than be abruptly woken from her sleepwalk and he had also informed them that often these bouts of 'walking' could be attributed to some kind of disturbance or trauma that the walker might have suffered. Ran did not need to look very far to find the cause of tonight's disturbance, and inwardly he cursed not just Vicky but Lloyd as well.

Didn't the man know just how lucky he was—what he, Ran, would give to change places with him?

Sylvie was still trembling against his body, her eyes wide open and unseeing as she stood stiffly beside him, almost transfixed. Not wanting to risk waking her, Ran urged her gently towards his own bedroom, talking very quietly and softly to her, just as though she were still the girl he remembered.

'It's all right, Sylvie,' he assured her gently. 'Everything's all right… Come on, now…'

Obediently she moved, leaning on him slightly. If he

could get her into bed without her waking up he could sit with her to check that she was going to sleep on and then he could spend the rest of the night in one of the other rooms. In the morning... He started to frown. Too late to regret now the jealousy which had prompted him to speak so harshly to her earlier, but the sight of that suit, the knowledge of just how it would look on her body, had filled him with such furious jealousy that he had overreacted.

Tenderly Ran guided her into his bedroom and towards the bed. The light gown she was wearing was plain and white, in soft cotton. In it she looked almost like a girl...youthful...virginal...

He closed his eyes. The last thing he needed right now was to start thinking about—to start *remembering*. Forcing himself to suppress the thoughts, the memories and the emotions which were running riot inside him, he stopped to pick her up, intending to lay her down on the bed, but as he did so a dog fox out in the woodland beyond the garden howled to his mate; the sound carried into the bedroom on the still night air, shocking him into immobility and Sylvie into immediate wakefulness.

'Ran...what...?'

He could hear the shocked anxiety in her voice as she stared round his moonlit bedroom.

'You were sleepwalking.' He tried to reassure her. 'I heard a noise...found you on the landing...'

Sleepwalking. Sylvie focused distractedly on Ran's face.

It had been years since she had last walked in her sleep, but she didn't for one moment doubt that Ran was telling the truth. After all, there was no reason why he should have spirited her from her own bed and carried her here to his—was there? If he had wanted to take her there, all he had to do... But even so... She started to shiver.

She only walked in her sleep in times of intense personal stress...intense personal *dis*tress...

'It's all right, Sylvie,' she heard Ran saying gently. He was still holding onto her. Sylvie could feel the warmth of his arms, his body through the robe he was wearing and through her own fine cotton nightgown. Bemusedly she looked at him, her eyes huge and shadowed in the small oval of her pale face.

Outside a peafowl, one of the small colony which had migrated from Haverton Hall to the Rectory, its slumber no doubt disturbed by the mating call of the fox, screamed loudly, causing Sylvie to go rigid with tension.

'It's all right, Sylvie,' Ran repeated soothingly. 'It's only a peafowl.'

She knew that, of course—their noise was, after all, familiar to her—but for once she felt too weak to bother arguing the point with Ran.

His bedroom was on the opposite side of the house from hers and furnished very differently, with heavy early Georgian furniture that looked imposingly traditional and masculine. The room suited Ran, she thought abstractedly; it suited his maleness, his completeness. A wave of longing swept over her. Unable to stop herself, she turned in towards his body, lifting her hand towards him.

Later she wasn't even sure if she had actually *meant* to touch him or if the gesture had simply been one of longing, but as he turned his head towards her her fingertips grazed his mouth. She felt his breath against them, warm, tormenting her with all that could never be.

She started to look away and then, to her shock, she felt
Ran taking hold of her wrist, circling it with his thumb
and fingers, holding her hand where it was whilst he very
deliberately pressed a kiss to each of her fingertips in
turn.

Wild-eyed, Sylvie watched him, almost forgetting to
breathe in her shock.

'Ran,' she protested half-heartedly, but as she said the
word she was already moving closer to him, instinctively
seeking the warmth and the comfort of his body heat,
his body.

If it felt like heaven to have his arms close around
her, that was nothing compared to what it felt like to
have him lift his hands to her face and cup it whilst he
oh, so gently kissed her mouth, a slow, tender, lingering
kiss...a *lover's* kiss. Silently Sylvie pressed even closer
to him, lifting her own arms to hold him, her mouth and
then her whole body, trembling with the effort it took
her not to give in to what she was feeling.

She could feel her eyes fill with tears, feel them, too,
starting to flood over and roll down her face.

'Sylvie.' She could hear the emotion in Ran's voice
as he lifted one fingertip to touch them. 'Don't
cry...please don't cry. *No* man is worth your tears...'

'It just hurts so much,' Sylvie told him, unable to hold
back what she was feeling any longer. Somehow the
night and their seclusion had stripped away the barriers
she had fought so hard to erect against her love for him.

'I hate feeling like this,' she whispered. 'I hate loving
so much and so...so...unwontedly... It's so demeaning
and it hurts so badly.'

She heard Ran groan as though something about her
agonised and honest admission touched him very deeply

and then he was holding her, rocking her in his arms as he told her huskily, 'You mustn't be hurt, Sylvie. Please, don't be hurt…'

And then, totally unexpectedly, he was kissing her, not with the gentle tenderness he had shown her before, but with a fierce sensual passion that took her breath away and with it all her resistance. Her body went weak, pliable, compliant, yearning towards his as his mouth moved demandingly on hers. She could feel the fierce, heavy thud of his heart, the sudden swift betraying arousal of his body.

He was and always had been a very male man, she reminded herself. He might not love her, she might not be the woman he wanted, but she was here in his arms, loving him, wanting him, and she could sense how little it would take to overturn his self-control.

Swiftly, dangerously, stabbing right at the most intimate female heart of her, came the thought that she might never have his love but she could have tonight…her memories and perhaps even more. A woman alone need not feel ashamed to give birth to a child these days…she need not even name its father… A child…*Ran's* child… Already she was responding to him, inviting him, inciting him, her hands reaching out to move under his robe, shaping the hard muscles of his shoulders, his arms.

This time when the peafowl cried neither of them paid any attention to it. Beneath the insistent thrust of Ran's tongue, Sylvie's lips parted.

She just wanted comfort, that was all, Ran warned himself as he felt her mouth tremble beneath his. She didn't want him…love him…

But it was already too late. He wanted her, he loved

her, and, God forgive him, he couldn't stop himself from giving in to his need to show her all that a man's love for a woman could and should be.

He kissed her face, her throat, her shoulders as he slid the soft whiteness of her nightdress from her body, only partially managing to stifle his groan of longing as he looked at her clad only in moonlight.

Beneath Ran's heavy-lidded gaze, Sylvie felt her will-power melting. He wanted her; she could see it in his eyes, feel it in the fierce tremble of his fingertips as they traced the outline of her body. Even with her eyes closed, she could feel how much he wanted her.

Shakily Sylvie mirrored his touch on his body, tracing the deep V left by the open neckline of his robe. When she touched the knot which secured the robe she lifted a love-dazed glance to his and commanded huskily, 'Take it off.'

Silently Ran did so, never removing his gaze from hers as the robe slid to the floor.

Before, the last time, the *only* time, she had been too caught up in the intensity of what was happening and her own needs and emotions to do anything more than register the fact that he was there, that his body was...*his*... But now, this time...

Like a gourmet examining a banquet, a sumptuous repast which had been set out before her, she studied every bit of him, feasting her eyes and her senses on him. He was magnificent...he was perfect...he was Ran. Her love, her life, the father of her child, their child... A fierce thrill ran through her.

'Ran.'

She said his name urgently, almost harshly. As she stepped towards him he stopped her, circling her wrists with his hands, holding her slightly away from him whilst he looked at her in turn. She could see the fierce hunger in his eyes as he focused on her breasts and an excited kick of pleasure gripped her.

There was something so dangerously erotic about standing there naked in front of him, her hands virtually pinioned, that it fed her own senses, her own need…to the point where she could feel her arousal beating a heavy pulse of longing so strongly within her body that she was forced to surrender to it.

Her eyes, soft with emotion, echoed the need, the feeling that was pulsing through her body, touching her, she felt, to her very soul as she looked deep into Ran's eyes. The huge wave of emotion that caught her up and rendered her powerless to do anything to withstand it contained far, far more than just physical desire or the immediacy of the moment. She felt a sense of fate, of destiny almost, as though all the previous emotions, all the love she had known for him had brought her here, to this moment. He might not share her love but he was here with her; she could see in his eyes that somehow something within him was aware of her and responsive to her, even if it was only man's most basic need for a woman that drove him, and against all logic and rational thinking Sylvie knew that what happened between them tonight would be something precious and almost sacred, that the child she now longed so deeply to conceive would be special and loved, so very, very loved.

Odd to think how fate worked, and she could see as clearly as though she were there the small pack of pills in the bathroom, still containing the ones she had accidentally omitted to take since her arrival in Derbyshire, not by design or plan and certainly not because she had

had any intention, any pre-warning that this was going to happen.

'You're beautiful, do you know that?' she heard Ran declaring rawly as, still holding her wrists, he leaned forward and slowly kissed her face, her eyelids, her lips, each one in turn, with something that was almost reverence. Then he moved on to her throat…her breasts…before releasing her wrists and scooping her up in his arms as though he couldn't bear not to have the full length of her held tightly against his body any longer. He slid his hand into her hair and opened her mouth with a kiss so intense and passionate that Sylvie felt as though she was dissolving into him, becoming a part of him.

Just how long they stood like that, how long they kissed, she had no idea; all she did know was that when his mouth finally lifted from hers the room was full of the charged sound of their breathing, the oxygen content of the air somehow diminished so that she felt positively light-headed and dizzy, aching from head to foot with need and longing.

But Ran was ignoring her body language, her silent plea for the intimacy of his body weight lying heavily and sensuously against hers on the bed behind her. Instead he was picking her up and gently placing her on the bed.

'It's all right,' she heard him saying softly to her. 'Everything's all right.' And he was cupping her feet in his hands, slowly massaging them so that tingles of sensation and heat shot through her veins like liquid fire. The feeling of his lips brushing her toes, so unexpected and shockingly intimate, made her gasp in shock, but when she instinctively tried to pull away he stopped her, his tongue weaving a rainbow patter of sensation against her skin as he caressed her toes, the narrow indentation of her fine-boned ankles, the exquisitely sensitive place just behind her knees and then the soft, quivering flesh of her thighs. All of them felt the slow, lingering touch of his mouth whilst the heat of an arousal so intense that she could hardly endure it covered her body in a soft sheen of reaction to what he was doing.

Only when she heard him groan as her thighs trembled in involuntary and uncontrollable response to his touch did she feel him remove his mouth from her, and only then did she realise too that the sound she could hear, had heard, whilst he caressed her was the raw, sobbed sound of her own breathing.

'Ran...'

Unable to stop herself, she moaned his name with all her pent-up need and longing openly displayed, but although he raised his head and looked sombrely at her, although she could see quite plainly as he moved the evidence of his own need, his response to her wasn't to cover her, to move over her and within her as she so longed for him to do, but instead to slide his hands along her thighs, holding, parting, lifting them and then moving round her. His thumbs traced the V between her thighs, following the line of soft hair that grew there before he buried his head against her, breathing in her scent, moaning her name over and over again as he caressed her sex with his tongue and his lips.

The hot molten weight of her own need completely swamped her. The pulse she had felt before had become a thunderous roar, an avalanche of frantic need that gathered and tightened until it overwhelmed her completely, exploding inside her in a series of sharp bursts of pleasure that left her trembling and panting, dizzy and elated, and yet somehow not quite fully satisfied…not complete. She was driven instead to reach for Ran, to cover him with kisses as she drew him closer to her, his torso, where his body hair felt slick and damp with his passion, his throat, where he groaned as she ran her tongue-tip hungrily over his Adam's apple, his jaw, his ears, his mouth.

Fiercely she wrapped herself around him. Her arms, her legs, holding him in an embrace that went back to Eve, knowing instinctively that he would be unable to resist it…or her…

The feeling of him moving against her was just as she remembered it only more intense, like comparing a faded photograph to the sharp colours of reality. Sylvie caught her breath on a cry of primal female pleasure as he moved within her, her body urging him deeper, her eyes liquid with emotion as she whispered to him how much she wanted him, how much she needed him.

'Yes, Ran, yes,' she said, twisting and turning, volubly as well as physically inviting him to possess her as deeply and intimately as only a woman in love did invite a man.

Instinctively she knew that what they were experiencing and sharing went far, far beyond mere sex, that each thrust of his body within hers brought them both ever closer to eternity, to creation itself.

As she felt her body open up completely to receive him, Sylvie gripped him tightly, her eyes open wide, fixed intently on his as she begged him, 'Now, Ran; let it be now…'

And as he responded to her, as she felt the hot liquid pulse of his release within her, her own cycle of rhythmic orgasmic contractions began again, only this time they were so much deeper and stronger; this time they weren't for mere pleasure, she decided, half dazed with the intensity of what she was experiencing. This time they were harvesting the gift he had given her, the precious gift of life.

As his body subsided within hers, Ran still held her, stroking her hair, brushing his lips against her forehead, whilst she breathed in the hot, satisfied male scent of his skin.

'It's been a long time,' she heard him saying unevenly as his heartbeat still thundered against her body.

'Yes,' she agreed quietly. There was no need for her to lie, to pretend; even if it was only temporarily, the barriers between them had been swept to one side by what she had experienced. Oddly she almost felt proud of the truth, of loving him so intensely that she had never been able to share herself with anyone else.

'I'm not... Sex for sex's sake just isn't for me...'

There was a brief silence. She lifted her head and looked uncertainly at Ran. What was he thinking? Was he wishing she had been less open and honest, that she had pretended that what they had just shared meant nothing, that *he* meant nothing? But when she looked into his eyes they were too dark for her to be able to read his expression properly. All she could see was his faintly twisted smile before he touched her face gently and told her, 'I meant that it had been as long a time for *me*, Sylvie...that I hadn't...couldn't... I was trying to explain...to excuse the fact that...that I wasn't as controlled as I should have been.'

'You were...you felt good to me,' Sylvie told him

simply and truthfully, compelled to add, 'But then, I don't have…you have…'

'Been less thankfully in control on either of the occasions we've been like this…?' Ran suggested ruefully. 'You're very kind, Sylvie, and…' His body suddenly tensed and when he moved she could see in his eyes something that made her own stomach muscles lock in sensual expectation.

'And I'm afraid I am likely to give you another demonstration of just how lacking in self-control you make me,' he told her with a soft groan as he took hold of her hand and placed it on his body, commanding her huskily, 'Feel.'

Instinctively Sylvie let her touch become a soft caress, her heart thudding as she felt him grow and harden still further beneath her fingertips.

'Oh, God, Sylvie, Sylvie,' she heard him protest, and he took hold of her, kissing her passionately as their bodies immediately and instinctively moved closer together.

It was fully daylight when Sylvie eventually woke up, her face flushing with hot colour as she opened her eyes to find Ran propped up on one elbow watching her.

'How long have you been awake?' she asked him, nervously clutching hold of the bedclothes, her colour deepening as she started to remember in full the events of the previous night.

'Long enough to know that you snore,' Ran told her ungallantly.

'Snore? I do *no* such thing,' Sylvie protested indignantly, letting go of the duvet in her ire.

'No? Well, then, you growl…' Ran teased her.

'I do not growl! I don't make *any* kind of noise at all,' Sylvie protested.

'Oh, yes, you do,' Ran told her immediately, his manner completely changing, the amusement in his eyes replaced by a look of shockingly burning intensity as he leaned closer to her and half whispered against her mouth as his fingertips brushed the tip of her breast.

'When I touch you here you make a little sound deep in your throat, and...'

'No. No, I don't want to listen to any of this,' Sylvie cried out frantically as the full reality of her situation hit her.

Last night she and Ran had made love...last night she had ignored all the rules, all the laws of dignity and common sense and self-preservation which she had sworn she would adhere to, and...

And last night, lost in the fathomless deep waters of love and longing, she had prayed that she might conceive Ran's child, had prayed for it and ached for it. A deep shudder racked through her. Logic told her that it was far too soon for her, for *anyone*, to know that she had done so, but somehow she did; somehow she sensed that already the seed that would be Ran's child was growing there, implanted deep within her.

Immediately tears filled her eyes, tears of love for the child she knew would be her whole life, and tears also for the fact that he would never know the love of his father, for already she had decided that this child must be *her* child, *her* responsibility, that Ran must never know of its existence, that her child must not be a child whose father only acknowledged him out of duty, a child who knew that its mother was not and never had been loved by its father.

'You're crying.' She could hear the accusation in Ran's voice and immediately tried to blink away her tears. 'I'm sorry about last night,' she heard Ran telling her gruffly. 'I *do* understand... It must be hard for you loving a man who doesn't...'

'Love me back,' Sylvie supplied chokily for him. If, in the past, she had thought that his anger and contempt were hard to bear, they were nothing now that she was faced with his pity and compassion. 'Yes. It is,' she agreed. 'But I'm a woman now, Ran, not a child, and if I choose to love the wrong person, then that is my choice and my *right*. The last thing I want or need is your pity,' she told him sharply, pride making her hold up her head.

'Last night shouldn't have happened,' Ran told her quietly, 'but I...'

'Couldn't help yourself,' Sylvie finished lightly. 'Yes, so you said at the time. It's obviously something we should both...forget...'

Sylvie looked away as she spoke, knowing quite well that she was lying, that she would have the most important reason there could be for *not* forgetting it, for not being *able* to forget it, but that wasn't a piece of information she had any intention of sharing with Ran.

'I...I should like to go back to my own room to get dressed before Mrs Elliott arrives,' she told him with formal dignity, adding, when he continued to look at her, 'I want you to turn your back, Ran, so that I can get out of this bed...'

The look he gave her made her face burn.

'Yes, I know that you've already seen...that... But that was last night,' she snapped self-consciously. 'That was then...this...this is now; this is different...'

'Yes, it is, isn't it?' Ran agreed heavily, and then, to

her relief, he turned away so that she could slip out of
the bed and snatch up her nightdress which she pulled
on before heading for the door, opening it without pausing to look back because she knew that if she did look
back—

Last night had been the most perfect, the most wonderful night of her life, but now it was over and soon,
too, with Lloyd's agreement, her time here would be
over, and only *she* would know that when she left
Haverton Hall, when she left *Ran*, she would be carrying
a small and very precious piece of him with her.

CHAPTER 10

'I'M SORRY to disturb you but Ran said that he thought you might like coffee.'

Forcing a welcoming smile to her lips, Sylvie took the tray from Ran's housekeeper.

She had been working in the library all morning, painstakingly going through the accounts and costings for the work she had already commissioned for Haverton Hall.

But now, even though she hadn't eaten any breakfast and she knew that she ought to be hungry, the *only* hunger she had was the never-ending hunger for Ran's love. And, as he had made more than plain to her, that was something she could never have.

Half an hour later she was just on her way downstairs, intending to drive over to Haverton, when her mobile rang. Answering it, she was surprised to hear Lloyd's voice on the other end of the line.

'Lloyd. I wasn't expecting to hear from you today. I thought you'd be...otherwise engaged,' Sylvie told him tactfully.

'Well, I guess I thought I would be too,' she heard Lloyd responding with a rueful note in his voice. 'Like they say, though, there's no fool like an old fool. Still, it was fun while it lasted, and I guess I had my money's worth.'

From the tone of his voice Sylvie immediately recognised that Lloyd had quickly become disillusioned with Vicky.

'I'm going to miss you, hon, when I'm back in New York,' Lloyd told her with the warm affection that was so much a part of his personality.

'I'll miss you as well,' Sylvie told him gravely, and meant it. 'Lloyd, I need to talk to you,' she added quietly. 'There's…there's… I can't stay here… I…I want to come back to New York…'

Biting down hard on her bottom lip, Sylvie willed herself not to lose control. Lloyd would wonder what on earth was the matter with her. She hadn't intended to blurt it all out like that. She had told herself that she would wait, assemble all her arguments and then talk to him calmly and quietly, and yet here she was, letting her emotions run away with her, giving in to the urgent need she felt to protect herself from the pain that being so physically close to Ran was causing her.

'Say, honey, you sound upset. What's wrong?' she heard Lloyd asking her anxiously.

'I can't discuss it over the phone,' Sylvie told him. 'I need to see you… Oh, Lloyd, I'm so sorry…' She gulped as she heard her voice thickening with tears.

'Don't be,' she heard Lloyd telling her gently, and then, to her relief, he said, 'I'll be there with you just as soon as I can fix up everything down here and then we can talk.'

'Oh, Lloyd,' Sylvie wept.

How typical it was of Lloyd that he should put everything else on hold to come and see her, Sylvie acknowledged after their call had ended. He would understand, she knew he would, but she still felt guilty about letting him down.

The door to Ran's study was open and Ran himself entered the hallway just as she was about to cross it. As he glanced at the mobile she was still holding in her hand, Sylvie realised that he must have overheard her talking to Lloyd.

'Lloyd's coming back,' she told him huskily.

'Yes, so I gathered,' she heard him responding flatly, with something that almost sounded like anger hardening his voice. Sylvie couldn't bring herself to look at him. Already the tenderness they had shared last night felt as though it was all something she herself had imagined, created out of her own need; it had gone.

'I…I have to go to Haverton,' she told him shakily as she made to walk past him.

Ran watched her go. It tore him apart to see the pain she was in. Last night she had turned to him in need, in simple human need, driven by her longing, her *love* for another man, a man who had left her to be with another woman.

Did Lloyd have any conception of what he had done, of what he *was* doing, or did he simply think that his wealth gave him the right to ignore other people's feelings? Did he think that the damage he had done to Sylvie, the hurt he had caused her, simply didn't matter?

Yesterday he had left her to be with someone else and now, today, he was coming back.

'I need to see you,' he had heard Sylvie whisper emotionally to him, and as he had heard the betraying tremble in her voice he had closed his eyes. He knew all about that need, had known about it from long before the night he had taken Sylvie in his arms in a mixture of fury and longing, breaking every promise he had ever made himself as he made love to her, *with* her, and discovered, with a mixture of joy, pain and shame, that he was her first lover.

'Wayne's been telling me for ages to find someone to lose my virginity with,' she had thrown tauntingly at him, and she had gone from him to Wayne, abandoning everything and everyone to be with him—her family, her education, even, it had seemed to Ran at times, her principles.

But then she had changed her mind, begged Alex for his help and support, to help her get her life back on track.

He had seen her off at the airport with Alex and his new wife, an impulse decision, giving in to a need for which he had berated and despised himself.

He had ended up going home afterwards and slowly getting drunk—not something he was in any way proud to remember, but it had been the only way he could find to anaesthetise himself against his pain.

Not even to Alex, his closest friend, had he been able to talk about how he felt, about how much he loved her. Alex was, after all, her stepbrother.

He had thought that he was prepared for the reality of knowing that she would spend her life with someone else, but that had been when that reality was at a safe distance. Knowing she loved Lloyd was one thing; having to witness that love, having to hold her whilst she cried for him, having to listen to her pleading with him for his return—no amount of preparation could protect him from that kind of pain.

And now Lloyd was on his way back to see her. Would she tell him about last night, about the intimacy *they* had shared? Morally there was no reason why she should do so but...

Last night, when he had held her, touched her, loved her, when he had felt her body's response to him, answered not just its sensuality but its deeper and far more intensely urgent demand for something that went far beyond even the physical, sexual satisfaction he had felt...known... He opened his eyes and walked across to the window of his study to look out into the garden. Long-ago ancestors of his had designed and planned this garden, lived in this building; his title, his land, the great house which was now too big and too expensive for any one family to run—all that tradition now rested on him and with him.

Once, long ago, it would have been considered his duty as the last male of his line to produce a child, a son, a legitimate heir. But that was something he could never do. He could not marry another woman when it was Sylvie he loved, not for his own sake and not for any wife's either, so there would be no legitimate heir. The only child he would ever have was the one he knew already that he and Sylvie had created between them last night. *Their* child. But he could not compel Sylvie to allow him to be a part of that child's life. Not when he knew that she didn't love him. Twice now she had turned to him for comfort when, in reality, she had loved another man. There could not, must not ever be a third occasion.

Lloyd was more than likely to arrive before evening and Ran knew that he simply could not endure being there to see him reunited with Sylvie.

He walked back to his desk and reached for the telephone.

In the pretty sitting room which his wife had made so much her own, Alex grinned in appreciation as their son headed eagerly towards him, swinging him up into his arms as Mollie looked on placidly. Alex looked lovingly at her. She was in the early stages of pregnancy with their second child and suffering from morning sickness.

'I've just had a phone call from Ran,' he told her.

'Mmm… How is he—and Sylvie…?'

'He wants to come down for a few days. Apparently he wants to pick my brains for ideas on making the estate more self-sufficient.'

'Do you think he and Sylvie will ever work things out?' Mollie asked him anxiously.

Alex raised his eyebrows.

'Why ask me? *You're* the one who thinks that they are madly in love with one another.'

'I don't *think*, I *know*,' Mollie corrected him sternly. 'But the pair of them are just so…so stubbornly determined not to admit to one another how they feel.'

'Has it ever occurred to you that you might *just* be wrong?' Alex asked her tenderly.

'No, because I'm not. You're Sylvie's brother, Alex, and Ran's best friend; you have a duty to do something to help them.'

'Oh, no! No! No way…' Alex denied, shaking his head and looking alarmed. 'They are both adults.'

'Maybe. But they're both behaving like children. We have to do *something*, Alex; you *saw* the way Sylvie was breaking her heart over Ran when we went to see her in New York just after she went there… It was pitiful to see the look in her eyes when she finally managed to ask after him… And Ran's just as bad.'

'Look, they're at Haverton Hall together…alone,' Alex stressed. 'If that doesn't give them both the opportunity to sort themselves out…'

'Maybe being alone isn't what they need, maybe they need someone to talk to, to show them…' Mollie suggested meaningfully, giving him a coaxing smile.

'No way,' Alex told her firmly, but Mollie had made up her mind. One way or another, something would have to be done, and if Alex couldn't be persuaded to do that something, well, then—

Determinedly she started to think.

It was later in the afternoon when Sylvie returned from Haverton Hall to learn from Mrs Elliott that Ran had announced that he had to go away for several days.

'Did he say where he was going or when he would be back?' Sylvie asked her stiffly.

The older woman shook her head.

'He just said that he would telephone,' she informed her.

Had Ran genuinely gone away on business or had he gone because of *her*? Sylvie wondered painfully. He had been kind towards her when he had talked about the pain of unrequited love, kinder than she had ever known him be before, but that didn't alter the fact that he didn't love her and that her presence here in his home must be creating problems for him. Well, she wouldn't be creating those problems for very much longer, she decided, her determination to convince Lloyd to hand over their Haverton Hall project to someone else even stronger than it had already been.

Lloyd himself rang whilst she was upstairs updating her files, explaining that he had been delayed a little longer than he had expected and that it would be late evening before he arrived in Derbyshire.

Ran had instructed his housekeeper to prepare a room for Lloyd before he had left—the room next to her own, Sylvie discovered, when Mrs Elliott, the housekeeper, informed her of Ran's instructions.

Her mobile rang and she answered it, expecting to hear Lloyd's voice but hearing instead that of her step-sister-in-law.

'Mollie, how are you?' she asked, genuinely pleased to recognise her caller.

'Queasy,' Mollie responded, but Sylvie could tell from the happiness in the other woman's voice just how pleased she was about her recently announced pregnancy.

'Just you wait until it's your turn,' Mollie warned her. 'It's no joke. We had salmon for supper and it's my favourite and I couldn't touch a bite…'

Her turn! Sylvie gripped her mobile tightly. How would Mollie and Alex react when she told them that she was pregnant? They would want to know who the father of her child was, of course, although both of them were modern enough, *loving* enough, to accept her decision to keep the father's identity to herself and to bring up her child alone.

'How are things going up there?' Mollie asked her. 'How are you and Ran getting on…?'

To Mollie's intuitive ears the silence that hummed down the wire between them before Sylvie answered her spoke volumes.

'We aren't,' Sylvie told her shortly. 'And in fact…' She paused and then decided there was little point in keeping her decision from Mollie who was, in many ways, despite the distance which separated them, probably her closet friend; not just a stepsister-in-law.

'I…I've decided to ask Lloyd to take me off this project, Mollie. I can't…it isn't… My being here just isn't going to work… Ran and I…' She stopped.

'You still love him, don't you?' Mollie asked her gently.

For a moment Sylvie didn't think she was going to be able to reply but almost against her will she felt compelled to respond honestly to Mollie's gentle question.

'Yes. Yes, I do,' she admitted. 'More than ever. He's...he's everything I've ever wanted, Mollie. The *only* man I've ever loved, the only man I ever *will* love...in every sense of the word,' she admitted in a very low voice. 'There hasn't... I haven't... Isn't it incredible in this day and age,' she continued, her voice full of angry despair, 'that at my age the only man I've ever been intimate with, the only man who's ever touched me...made *love* to me...is Ran? And both times... He doesn't love me, Mollie. I *know* that. He never has, and that first time he was angry, and his reactions were... Both of us were angry and what we did...what we had... But this time it was so...so loving...so tender...so meaningful. But in reality he was just comforting me... He—'

'Did he *tell* you that?' Mollie interrupted her softly.

'Not in so many words. He talked about how painful it is to love someone who can't love you back, and...and about how there's no need to...to feel ashamed of having that love; of needing that person.

'I can't stay here, Mollie,' she burst out passionately. 'I'm afraid of what might happen, of what I might say...do... Ran was so kind, so...gentle and tender... I want to keep that memory... I don't want...'

'He must feel something for you if...'

'If he took me to bed?' Sylvie supplied dryly for her. 'He *wanted* me, yes, but... Lloyd was up here and he took Ran's latest lady-friend back to London with him. Oh, I don't think their relationship was particularly serious, but obviously Ran's a man, and as such...'

'He took you to bed because he wanted sex; is that what you're saying?' Mollie asked her shrewdly.

'Well, I think that was a large part of it,' Sylvie agreed.

'But he must have felt something for you, Sylvie, to talk to you the way you say he did. If he really didn't care, didn't *want* to get involved, then surely the last thing he would do would be to allow that kind of intimacy to take place between you.'

'Yes... No... Oh, I don't know. I just know... I just know that I'm afraid if I stay here I'll... I can't cope with it, Mollie; it's safer for me to put as much distance as I can between us...'

'Have you told him you're leaving?' Mollie asked her.

'Not in so many words,' Sylvie admitted. 'He knows that I've asked... Lloyd's coming up to Derbyshire to see me, but Ran isn't here at the moment. His housekeeper says he told her that he's had to go away for a few days, but he hasn't told her where or when he'll be back... I suspect that he's trying to avoid me...'

'Just like he was when he took you to bed,' Mollie suggested wryly. 'Have you ever asked him how he feels about you, Sylvie?'

For a moment Sylvie was too shocked to answer.

'No! No, of course not—I *couldn't*. How could I? Would you have asked Alex that?'

'Perhaps not,' Mollie acknowledged. 'But Alex's and my relationship is very different to yours and Ran's. We hadn't known one another very long. Whilst you and Ran...'

'The difference is that you and Alex love one another, whilst Ran and I... I have to go, Mollie. I just can't talk about it any longer,' Sylvie told her emotionally.

As she ended the call she prayed that Lloyd would get here soon. God and Lloyd willing, she could leave Derbyshire before Ran came back.

As though on cue she saw the lights of a car drawing

up outside the house, sweeping across her bedroom window. Lloyd at last...

Taking a deep breath, she went downstairs to meet him.

Half an hour later, after she had told Lloyd everything, he gravely handed her a handkerchief and asked her, 'You really love him that much?'

'Too much. Stupid, aren't I?' Sylvie said shakily, reiterating urgently, 'Lloyd, I hate letting you down, but I *can't* stay here—not now.'

'You aren't letting me down, honey. Your happiness means an awful lot to me. I guess I kinda think of you as the daughter I've never had. If I didn't have this meeting I'd wait to take you back with me.'

'No. No, you can't do that. I'll tie up all the loose ends I can whilst Ran's away. The least I can do is to leave everything in order for whoever takes over from me here.'

'See you in New York, then, hon,' Lloyd told her before taking her in his arms and hugging her.

A little later he had gone. Soon she would be gone too...

Her throat tight, Sylvie blinked away her tears.

CHAPTER ELEVEN

'IT's a beautiful spot here, isn't it?' Mollie commented as she walked across the grass to join Ran where he stood studying the pool in the centre of the small tree-filled glade.

Once, before her marriage to Alex, this glade had been the scene of disturbing desecration when it had been taken over by a band of travellers, eco-warriors, led by the drug dealer Wayne, who had convinced a then idealistic and innocent Sylvie that his sole object in travelling was to assert the rights of the homeless.

It had been Sylvie who had brought them to this pretty glade on her stepbrother's land, and ultimately Sylvie who had played a major part in the drama which had unfolded when she had realised just how dangerous and unsavoury a character Wayne actually was.

It had taken months to restore the glade to what it had once been. Now it was a favourite spot for local visitors. In the spring it was filled with the colour of hundreds and hundreds of bluebells, but now they were over and the trees were just beginning to show the beginnings of the turn of colour which heralded the end of summer.

'It's hard to believe now just how much this place has been transformed,' Mollie remarked as she stood at Ran's side.

'I wish I'd seen Sylvie the day she fell into the mud when you were cleaning out the lake and you had to pull her out... How old was she then, Ran?'

172

'Seventeen,' he responded immediately, causing Mollie to give him a swift, thoughtful look.

'Mmm... When we were talking the last time Sylvie was home she mentioned how upset she was when her mother insisted that she had to leave Otel Place. She wanted to stay on here with Alex after his father's death, but her mother wouldn't permit it.'

'She was a young girl on the verge of womanhood. A bachelor household just wasn't the place for her.'

'Even though one of those bachelors was someone she loved very deeply, someone she has never stopped loving...someone she *still* loves very deeply?' Mollie suggested.

'Alex felt that it was best that she stayed with her mother,' Ran told her doggedly.

'I wasn't referring to *Alex*,' Mollie returned gently. 'It was because of her love for *you*, Ran, that Sylvie wanted to stay here.'

'She was a child,' Ran told her angrily, turning away from her so that she couldn't see his face. 'What did she know of...love? She was so young, Mollie, and I was just her brother's manager; I couldn't afford...'

'To let her see that you loved her back?' Mollie suggested softly.

Ran turned round and looked angrily at her.

'What I intended to say was that I couldn't afford to give her the kind of lifestyle she was used to, and even if I had been able to do so she was too young, for God's sake, a child still...'

'She wasn't a child at nineteen,' Mollie reminded him, adding more meaningfully, 'And you didn't treat her as one either, Ran. You and she were lovers,' she told him directly. 'You were her first lover, but you left her, let her—'

'*No! She* was the one who left me,' Ran told her fiercely. 'She told me herself that the only reason she'd given herself to me was because Wayne didn't want a virgin…and…'

'And you *believed* her?' Mollie derided him quietly.

Ran looked at her.

'She was saying goodbye to him when I arrived and if you'd seen her with him…'

'Looks can be deceptive,' Mollie pointed out. 'People can go to extraordinary lengths to conceal what they really feel if they believe that exposing those feelings could lead to them being rejected and hurt.

'After all,' she added quietly, '*you've* concealed the fact that you love Sylvie from her, haven't you?'

Immediately Ran tensed, his jaw tightening.

'Alex told you?' he demanded. 'That was supposed to be—'

'Alex hasn't told me anything,' Mollie assured him. 'He didn't need to tell me, Ran; I guessed.'

'How?'

'By knowing the kind of man you are and subtracting that from the way you behave towards Sylvie, and coming up with a figure that just doesn't add up, not unless you add another ingredient to it,' she told him with a small smile. 'Why don't you tell her how you feel…?'

'She knows,' Ran told her shortly. 'Look, Mollie, I appreciate your concern,' he said. 'Maybe once, as a child, a young woman, Sylvie did love me, but that's all changed now. She's not a young girl any more, she's an adult. There've been other men in her life, men who—'

'*What* other men?' Mollie challenged him, and then added boldly before he could answer, '*You* are the only lover Sylvie has ever had, Ran, the only one she's ever wanted...'

'No...that's not true,' Ran denied, but Mollie could see the way he changed colour, his face paling beneath his outdoor tan. 'She and Wayne were lovers and now she has Lloyd.'

'No,' Mollie denied firmly, and then added more gently, 'No, Ran. Wayne and Sylvie were *never* lovers. She told me that at the time and I know it was the truth. She's said very much the same thing since, very recently.'

'How recently?' Ran pounced, and then shook his head. 'This isn't about other men, other loves. I would still feel the same way about her no matter how many other men there'd been in her life, but I can't, *won't* impose either myself or my love on her. She loves Lloyd.'

'Yes, she does,' Mollie agreed, 'but she loves him as a friend, Ran, not as a man.'

'You wouldn't say that if you'd heard her talking to him on the phone as I did, pleading with him to see her...'

Mollie took a deep breath. Before following Ran out here to talk with him there had been certain limits she had imposed on her revelations, certain boundaries she had told herself she must not and would not cross, certain confidences she would not share, but now she knew that she was going to have to break that self-imposed sanction.

'Pleading with him to see her because she wants to be taken off the Haverton Hall project,' Mollie told him quietly. 'She's desperately afraid, Ran, afraid of the way she feels about you and afraid of... She told me herself that she just doesn't think she can take any more. She said it was impossible for her to do her work properly when all she could think about was you. She wants Lloyd to allow her to work on something else, something that doesn't involve her in any kind of contact with you… It's up to you, Ran,' she told him simply, 'If you love her…'

'I saw the way she reacted when Lloyd left her to go to London with Vicky,' Ran told her tersely.

'Lloyd has never been her lover, Ran,' Mollie reasserted. 'She doesn't love him in that way, but if you doubt my word, if you really want to know the truth, there's only one person you need to talk with, isn't there? If you don't believe me, Ran, then think about this: why should a woman, any woman, not just allow but encourage a man to make love to her when she has been deliberately celibate for years and when she believes that he cares nothing for her? Why, unless it's because her own emotions are so strong, so powerful, that they are outside her own control? Very few human emotions come into *that* kind of category, Ran.

'Oh, and by the way…' Mollie paused and turned round as she started to walk away from him. 'I nearly forgot. Sylvie telephoned last night. She's spoken to Lloyd and he's agreed that she can leave Haverton whenever she wishes. She's booked on a flight from London tomorrow.

'Sometimes, for a woman, just being loved isn't enough.

Sometimes we need more than an act of faith and sometimes we need to be told, shown, to see it, to hear it, touch it, taste it.'

'What's the matter with Ran?' Alex asked Mollie curiously half an hour later as he walked into her sitting room. 'I've just passed him on the lane; he said he was going back to Haverton. He said something urgent had come up.'

'Mmm...did he...?'

'Mollie...' Alex said perceptively. 'What's been going on? What have you—?'

'Oh...' Putting her hand to her mouth, Mollie got up and raced for the door.

Morning sickness—what a euphemism, Alex decided. Poor Mollie suffered from it all day. Sympathetically he went to follow her.

Her bags were packed, a note left for Ran explaining that someone else was going to take over her work, her files were all in order; there was nothing left for her to do other than get into her hire car and drive it to the airport. Still Sylvie couldn't quite bring herself to go.

Irresolutely she made her way upstairs, pausing outside Ran's bedroom. She had the house to herself. Mrs Elliott had left for the day. Impulsively she opened the door and went inside. The room was just as she remembered it from that single night she had spent here. She went over to the bed, smoothing a trembling hand over the pillow which had been Ran's.

Tears burned behind her eyes but she refused to shed them. Instead she walked determinedly towards the door and through it.

Outside the air was warm with the heat of the late summer sun. She could see the lavender which grew in huge drifts alongside the drive.

Silently she turned to give one last look at the house. Where Haverton was a mansion, this was a true home. Very gently she touched the warm mellow brick before wheeling round and hurrying unsteadily towards her hire car. She had booked herself into a London hotel overnight ready for her morning flight to New York. It was time for her to leave. There was, after all, no reason for her to stay.

All the way north as he drove, Ran told himself that he was a complete fool, that Mollie was wrong.

'If Sylvie does love me, there's nothing to stop her saying so,' he had told Mollie sharply.

'Nothing, apart from the fact that she believes you don't love *her*,' Mollie had agreed.

Did she believe that? How *could* she? Only the other night, holding her in his arms, he had indirectly referred to his feelings for her.

His body ached with tension and the sense of urgency which had driven him north, not allowing him to pause or stop. The hills basked in the heat of the late afternoon sunshine as he drove the last few miles home.

He saw the Discovery before he saw her, his heart giving a huge leap of relief when he saw that it was still there, that *she* was still there. And then he saw her.

She was wearing the smart cut trouser suit and carrying her document case. Instinctively he pressed his foot down harder on the accelerator.

Ran was travelling at such a speed that at first Sylvie couldn't make out the shape of the car, never mind the driver, for the clouds of dust that surrounded it, but instinctively she knew it was Ran and immediately, for some idiotic reason, her first impulse was to get away before he saw her. But as she tugged frantically at the huge Discovery's door Ran was already bringing his car to a swerving halt in front of her, blocking her exit. He

got out of the car and strode towards her, his face grim
and unreadable.

'Ran... I...I was just leaving... I—'

'Why?' he demanded, cutting across her husky, nervous words.

'Why?'

'Why are you leaving, Sylvie? Is it because of Lloyd?
Because he's your lover and you can't bear to be away
from him...?'

Sylvie was too shocked to prevaricate.

'No!' she exclaimed immediately. 'Lloyd isn't my
lover.'

'Then why the hell were you so upset when he took
Vicky off to London with him?' Ran exploded.

'I... She... It was obvious what she was doing, how
mercenary she is, but you defended her, you encouraged
her to flirt...you praised her...you...'

'I couldn't wait for her to take Lloyd out of the way
so that you could see just how undeserving of you he
is,' Ran finished quietly for her.

Sylvie stared at him. The sun was shining down hotly
on her head, which must be the reason she was feeling
so peculiar, she decided dizzily. There could be no other
explanation for the look she had just imagined she had
seen in Ran's eyes.

'You can't really have thought that Lloyd and I were
lovers,' she told him shakily. 'He's my friend. I like
him... love him, yes, as a person, but...' She stopped
and wet her suddenly dry lips with the tip of her tongue.

'Don't do that, Sylvie,' she heard Ran demanding
rawly. 'Come with me,' he commanded, suddenly reaching out and taking hold of her hand before she could
stop him, hurrying her across the gravel and into a part

of the garden she had not explored as yet, down a yew-enclosed alleyway.

Through a doorway in the yew hedge Ran guided her into a small secluded garden which was entirely planted with white roses, so many of them that their scent made Sylvie feel light-headed.

'My great-uncle planted these roses in memory of the only woman he loved. She died of pneumonia shortly before they were due to be married and this garden and his memories were all that he had left of her.

'I don't want memories to be all I ever have of you, Sylvie. I love you,' he told her rawly. 'I have *always* loved you and will *always* love you. I haven't told you before because I didn't feel I had the right... First you were too young, then there was Wayne, and then...'

'You love me...?' Sylvie stared at him in disbelief. 'But only the other night you told me that you didn't, couldn't...' she reminded him. 'You said that you knew how painful it was for me to love you but that—'

She stopped as she heard the sharp explosive sound he made.

'No,' he corrected her. 'What I was trying to say was how painful it was for *me* to love you knowing that you didn't love me back.'

For a moment they stared at one another in silence and then, uncertainly, as though she was afraid to believe what she was hearing, Sylvie lifted her hand to his face, her fingers shaking as they touched his skin.

'You love me, Ran? I didn't... I can't... I'm afraid to believe it just in case...' She stopped and pressed her lips together, trying to stop them from trembling.

'Oh, God, Sylvie, what have I done—what have *we* done?' Ran demanded hoarsely as he reached for her. 'I loved you when you were sixteen, when I had no *right* to have the kind of feelings I had for you; I loved you when you were seventeen and you almost drove me crazy with what you were so innocently offering me. I loved you when you were nineteen and you flung your virginity at me like a gauntlet, giving me your body but denying me your love.'

'I thought you hated me,' Sylvie whispered. 'You were so angry with me when I came to Otel Place with Wayne and the travellers.'

'That wasn't anger, it was jealousy,' Ran told her dryly. 'You'll never know how many, many times the only thing that kept you out of my bed was that "anger". It was either alienate you or...'

'Why didn't you...? Why didn't you take me to bed then? You must have known how much I wanted it, how much I wanted *you*,' Sylvie said.

'No. No, I didn't. Oh, yes, I knew you'd had a crush on me at one stage, but when I saw you with Wayne, when you told me that you wanted him...'

'I thought you were rejecting me. I had my pride, you know,' Sylvie told him ruefully. 'You'd pushed me away so many times before—'

'For your own sake,' Ran interrupted her. 'As your mother had already pointed out to me, I had nothing to offer you.'

'*Nothing*...?' Sylvie protested emotionally, her eyes shining with suppressed tears. 'You had *everything*, Ran, were *everything* to me...still are everything.'

As he took her in his arms and kissed her, white petals from the roses drifted down onto them both.

'Like confetti,' Ran said softly when he finally, reluctantly lifted his mouth from hers. 'Traditionally we should be married from the private chapel at Haverton Hall, but it's badly in need of restoration and I can't wait that long.' As he kissed her again he whispered against her mouth, 'Perhaps our first child can be christened there.'

Immediately Sylvie opened her eyes.

'You know...about that,' she guessed. 'You...you felt it too...'

'Yes,' Ran acknowledged. 'How could we have been such fools, Sylvie, so blind? Surely that alone should have told us both, shown us both. What we shared that night, what we *created*, could only have come from mutual love.'

'Yes,' Sylvie admitted huskily. 'I still can't quite believe it...' she added, brushing white rose petals off his arms. 'It's...it's still so... It's less than an hour since I thought that I'd be driving away from Haverton and you, for ever. What made you come back? What—?'

'You did,' he told her promptly, and then relented when he saw her face.

'Mollie talked to me...made me think...see...'

'Mollie? But she never said a word when she rang me—' Sylvie began indignantly, and then stopped. 'Oh, Ran,' she whispered, 'I can't bear to think how close we came to...to not having this...not having one another.'

'It wouldn't have ended here,' Ran comforted her.

'I don't know what Lloyd's going to say when I tell him that I've changed my mind and I want to stay at Haverton...'

'For ever,' Ran told her.

'For ever,' Sylvie agreed.

'Let's go inside,' Ran said abruptly, 'I want to hold

you…make love with you…*show* you how much I love you…how much I need you.'

Ten minutes later, as she lay in his arms on his bed, tracing the strong shape of his nose, she told him huskily, 'There's only ever been you, Ran. I couldn't bear…didn't want…'

'Do you think it's been any different for me?' he demanded rawly.

Uncertainly Sylvie looked at him.

'But you're a man,' she protested. 'There was always someone…one of your sophisticated women-friends…'

'*Friends*, yes,' Ran agreed, 'but lovers, no. Oh, I had some meaningless encounters in the early days, but I've not slept with anyone for a long time. It isn't so very much different for a man, Sylvie, not when he loves a woman the way I love you. Perhaps that was part of the reason why… Will it be a boy or a girl, do you think?'

'I don't know,' Sylvie answered. 'What I do know, though, is that he or she will be a creation of our love.'

'We shall have to marry quickly and quietly,' Ran told her. 'Your mother won't like that…'

'I'd like to be married at Otel Place,' Sylvie said softly. 'Where we first met. I do like this room, Ran,' she added dreamily. 'It's very you.'

'Do you? I'm very glad to hear that since from now on you're going to be seeing an awful lot of it,' Ran told her mock-solemnly before drawing her down against him and cupping her face so that he could kiss her.

They were married five weeks later at Otel Place with just their immediate family in attendance and, of course, Lloyd, whom Sylvie had especially wanted to be there.

Alex gave her away whilst her mother, who had been

overjoyed to discover that she was to marry Ran, sobbed into her handkerchief. Alex and Mollie's child was their only attendant, carrying the ring with solemn determination on a velvet cushion embroidered with Ran's family's arms. Sylvie's dress was cream and gold.

'White has never suited me,' she had told Mollie, adding, tongue-in-cheek, 'Besides, it wouldn't be appropriate.'

'I should hope not,' Mollie had agreed. 'After the years you and Ran have been apart, I'm surprised he let you out of bed long enough to *get* married,' she'd added forthrightly.

Sylvie had laughed and then asked demurely, 'What makes you think that he's the one keeping me in bed? I love him so much, Mollie,' she'd added seriously, 'and it's all thanks to you that we're together.'

'Well, don't try to repay me by naming this after me,' Mollie had warned her as she'd gently patted Sylvie's still flat stomach.

Sylvie had stared at her.

'You know? But how…? I…'

'I saw the colour you turned at breakfast the other morning,' Mollie had told her wryly. 'And besides… Well, let's just say that Ran has that certain look about him. He loves you so much, Sylvie.'

Involuntarily Sylvie's glance now went to her new husband, her heart starting to thud heavily. Much as she loved her family, right now the *only* person she wanted was Ran. Quietly she made her way towards where he was talking with Alex, linking her arm through his as she suggested softly, 'Let's go home, Ran…'

'I really think that Haverton is my favourite of all our buildings,' Lloyd confessed to Sylvie as they both stood together in the ante-chamber to the small family chapel where Sylvie and Ran's baby son and Lloyd's godson had just been christened.

'You say that about every one of them,' Sylvie teased, but Lloyd shook his head.

'No, Haverton *is* special,' he insisted. 'You've done a fine job here, Sylvie. Are you sure I can't tempt you to come back to work for me? There's a palace I've seen in Spain...'

'No.' Laughing, Sylvie shook her head. 'I have another project to occupy me now,' she reminded him, looking lovingly towards her son, who was being cradled by his father.

The work on Haverton had been finished just in time for Rory's christening. The official opening of the house to the public was scheduled for the end of the month.

Ran hadn't put any pressure on her to make her project on Haverton the last one. She *wanted* to be with Rory and, of course, with Ran. Maybe in years to come she might pick up her career again, although she doubted it. She was the Trust's official caretaker for Haverton, and looking after the house and its grounds was going to prove more than stimulating enough.

Already, even before the house officially opened, she had bookings for a string of weddings, carrying right through the coming year, never mind the conferences and private parties who had expressed interest in hiring the house. It was extremely satisfying to know that simply on the interest that had already been shown in the house her costings indicated that it would earn enough to pay for its own upkeep.

'Even if you had managed to run away from me,' Ran had told her only the previous night, 'sooner or later I would have seen Rory, and once I had I would have known that he was mine and then...'

'And then...?' Sylvie had demanded challengingly.

'And then I would have remembered how he came into being and then somehow I'd have found a way to become a part of his life— and yours,' Ran had told her quietly.

'Because he's your son?' she had asked him.

'Because you're my woman...my love...' Ran had corrected her.

Sometimes, even now, she couldn't believe how lucky she had been, how wonderful her life was. Living at the Rectory was fulfilling part of her childhood dream—the house so closely mirrored the secret home she'd used to create for herself. But it wasn't, of course, her home, wonderful though it was, that made her feel that she had been so especially blessed... She looked tenderly at Ran.

If the Rectory was her dream home then Ran was certainly her dream man, although to describe him as such in no way did either him or the depth and intensity of the love they shared true justice.

Ran was her man, her mate, her soul and the real heart of her life... Without him... Without him she wouldn't have her beautiful kitchen floor covered in mud as it had been the other morning when he had come in shouting triumphantly that the poachers he had suspected of taking their stock had finally been caught poaching from a neighbour's property.

She smiled secretly to herself. Rory was six months old and she suspected that well before he reached his second birthday he would have a sibling, a brother or a sister.

'What are you smiling for?' Ran asked her as he came

over to her with Rory and kissed her lovingly on the
mouth.

'You know that avenue of limes we planted at
Haverton to mark Rory's birth?'

'Mmm…'

'Well, do you remember you said that we'd plant a
cross walkway to mark the birth of our second child?'

'Mmm…'

'Well,' Sylvie told him with a twinkle in her eyes, 'I
think you'd better think about ordering saplings now…'

'Sylvie…?' Ran queried, but she was already turning
away from him to speak to someone else. 'Just you wait
until later,' he mock-growled in her ear, but as she answered the interested questions of one of his elderly
aunts about the restoration work on Haverton Ran
looked down into the alert eyes of his son and told him
softly, 'Something tells me you're going to have to get
used to the idea of being a big brother, Rory.'

HARLEQUIN ✦ PRESENTS®

WANTED: ONE
WEDDING DRESS

A trilogy by

Sharon Kendrick

**Three brides in search of the perfect
dress—and the perfect husband!**

In February 1999 wedding-dress designer
Holly Lovelace marries the man of her dreams in
One Bridegroom Required!
Harlequin Presents® #2011

In March 1999 Amber has her big day in
One Wedding Required!
Harlequin Presents® #2017

In April 1999 Ursula, Amber's sister,
walks up the aisle, too!
One Husband Required!
Harlequin Presents® #2023

Available wherever Harlequin books are sold.

✦ **HARLEQUIN**®
Makes any time special ™

Look us up on-line at: http://www.romance.net   HPWOWD

The Perfect Saga
from *New York Times*
bestselling author

The Crightons appear to have everything—
money, position, power and elegance...and
a past scandal to haunt them.

If you missed any of the books in the Crighton family
saga, act now to order your copies today!

Coming Next Month

HARLEQUIN PRESENTS®

THE BEST HAS JUST GOTTEN BETTER!

#2007 THE VENGEFUL HUSBAND Lynne Graham
(The Husband Hunters)

To claim her inheritance and save her home, Darcy needed a husband, *fast!* Her advertisement was answered by Gianluca Raffacani—and while *he* wasn't aware he was her child's father, *she* didn't know he wanted revenge....

#2008 THE SEXIEST MAN ALIVE Sandra Marton
(Valentine)

Finding the Sexiest Man Alive to feature in *Chic* magazine was Susannah's last hope to stop Matt Romano from taking it over. But Matt insisted on assisting her and seducing her. Was he the world's sexiest man...?

#2009 IN BED WITH THE BOSS Susan Napier

Duncan had never forgotten his one night of passion with his secretary, Kalera, even if she had. Now she was engaged to another man...and Duncan vowed to entice her back to *his* bed...for good!

#2010 EXPECTANT MISTRESS Sara Wood
(Expecting!)

Four years after their first brief affair, Adam and Trish were back together again, and she was wondering if this was another fling.... But before she could tell him she was pregnant with his baby, she received a fax from his fiancée....

#2011 ONE BRIDEGROOM REQUIRED! Sharon Kendrick
(Wanted: One Wedding Dress)

Holly had the dress; now she needed a groom! Then she met Luke who was perfect—except that he wanted an *un*consummated marriage! If Holly was to have the perfect wedding *night*, this virgin would have to seduce her husband!

#2012 A FORBIDDEN DESIRE Robyn Donald
(50th Book)

Paul McAlpine found Jacinta mesmerizing, and now they would be spending the whole summer together. But he had to resist her—after all, she was engaged to another man....